"Buck, there's something I need to tell you."

The despondent tone in Destiny's voice sent up a warning flag in Buck's head. Was she ready to come clean about the broken axle? Well, he wasn't ready to hear her confession—not after their kiss in the desert. "Go upstairs and rest. We'll talk later."

"But—"

He pressed his finger to her lips and swore he saw a spark in her blue eyes. There was definitely something happening between them, whether either of them were ready to admit it or not. She gave in and climbed the fire escape to the apartment above the garage. At the door she glanced over her shoulder, and the longing in her gaze stole the air from his lungs. Then she disappeared from view.

Buck had never been with a girl like Destiny—she was everything he'd never wanted in a woman—or so he'd thought anyway. There was no denying the Harley princess made his motor race. He wanted— no, *needed*—to take a walk on the wild side with her.

And let the chips fall where they may.

Dear Reader,

Welcome back to The Cash Brothers series! You've watched Johnny Cash fall in love with the girl next door, Conway Twitty Cash fall in love with his best friend and Willie Nelson Cash fall back in love with the girl he got pregnant in high school. Now it's time for Buck Owens Cash to find his lady love.

After Buck has a falling-out with his brother Will, he hits the rodeo circuit. But he doesn't get far because his truck breaks down. Buck finds himself at the mercy of a redheaded mechanic who rides a Harley and an old Route 66 town full of eccentric retirees. When their whirlwind ride on her Harley comes to a stop, Buck will never look at life the same way. And isn't that what love is all about? Seeing life in a new light—a light that leads down the road to happy ever after.

If you missed reading previous Cash Brothers books, *The Cowboy Next Door* (July 2013), *Twins Under the Christmas Tree* (October 2013) and *Her Secret Cowboy* (February 2014) are still available through online retailers. To find out more about my books and where I hang out on social media, please visit www.marinthomas.com.

And if you enjoyed this book I'd very much appreciate your help in spreading the word about The Cash Brothers series. The best way to do that is by leaving a short online book review at Goodreads, Amazon or Barnes and Noble, or by recommending this book to a friend or family member. Thank you for your support and help in building my readership one reader at a time!

Happy Ever After...The Cowboy Way

Marin

THE COWBOY'S DESTINY

—

Marin Thomas

HARLEQUIN® AMERICAN ROMANCE®

Recycling programs
for this product may
not exist in your area.

ISBN-13: 978-0-373-75519-6

THE COWBOY'S DESTINY

Printed in U.S.A.

ABOUT THE AUTHOR

Marin Thomas grew up in Janesville, Wisconsin. She left the Midwest to attend college in Tucson, Arizona, where she earned a B.A. in radio-TV. Following graduation she married her college sweetheart in a five-minute ceremony at the historic Little Chapel of the West in Las Vegas, Nevada. Over the years she and her family have lived in seven different states, but they've now come full circle and returned to Arizona, where the rugged desert and breathtaking sunsets provide plenty of inspiration for Marin's cowboy books.

Books by Marin Thomas

HARLEQUIN AMERICAN ROMANCE

To the 2013 members of The Cash Brothers Cowgirl Posse—Denise, Nancy, Susan, Teresa, Sabrina, Gaby, Renee, Linda H., Linda S., Kim, Granny and junior posse member Karlie—thank you for your friendship and the amazing support you give me and my books. You cowgirls rock!

Chapter One

Late Thursday afternoon Destiny Saunders stuck her finger beneath her borrowed wedding veil and scratched her prickly scalp.

Daryl Rivers, where are you?

She stared at the open chapel doors willing her fiancé to magically appear.

The bald, rotund minister, who had a habit of clearing his throat every ten seconds, wiped the top of his sweaty head with a handkerchief. The Sunset Desert Chapel did not have central air. A gust of hot August heat blew up the aisle, sending the lace veil soaring into the air.

"Perhaps you'd like to call your young man one more time?" the minister said.

She'd like to call her *young man* a name that began with a four-letter word. Destiny walked over to the pew where she'd set her purse and removed her cell phone then pressed three.

You've reached Daryl. I'm rockin' 'n' rollin'. Leave me a message.

"Daryl, where are you? We were supposed to get married thirty minutes ago. Call—" *Beeeep.* Ignoring the queasy feeling in her stomach she marched down the aisle and poked her head out the door. She didn't want to believe Daryl had stood her up.

The sound of a car engine met her ears and relief swept through her—but it was short-lived when she spotted the minister's Cadillac driving off.

And still she waited.

Waited and watched as the afternoon sun dropped lower in the Arizona sky. Her thoughts drifted to Lizard Gulch. What concerned her more than Daryl abandoning her was losing the town she'd grown to love—the one place she felt she belonged.

She fingered the frayed edges of the veil. Violet Hemp would be upset that she hadn't married. The older woman had offered the use of her 1950s headdress as the *something borrowed* part of Destiny's bridal outfit.

Blast you, Daryl.

Even though they'd known each other only six months, she hadn't expected him to leave her high and dry. She closed her eyes and recalled their first date. Daryl had taken her to a tattoo parlor in Kingman. And since she'd decided to call Lizard Gulch home, she'd gotten a colorful lizard tattooed on the back of her shoulder. Daryl had picked a two-headed snake for his arm. Afterward they'd stopped at the Sonic for shakes and that's when she'd discovered they had more in common than new tattoos—they'd both experienced crummy childhoods.

Destiny hadn't had any contact with her mother in ten years. She'd been thirteen when she'd walked out of the Tomahawk Truck Plaza in Phoenix with only the clothes on her back and ten dollars in her pocket. She rarely reflected on her childhood—growing up in truck stops where her mother entertained men in bathroom stalls wasn't the stuff of fairy tales.

She rubbed her belly. At barely two months pregnant it would be several weeks before she showed. Destiny admitted she didn't love Daryl, and he'd never confessed to loving her, but she'd believed they could make a go of a real marriage for the baby's sake.

Well, crap. Now what?

She retrieved her purse then left the chapel, closing the doors behind her. After stowing her purse and phone in the bench compartment of her 1980 Harley-Davidson Wide Glide hog, she slid on her mirrored sunglasses and straddled the seat, careful to keep her white leather pants from touching the greasy engine. She positioned the two-inch heel of her black biker boot over the kickstarter and jumped down on it with all her measly one hundred and ten pounds. The engine revved to life, and she flipped the stand up then tore out of the parking lot, tires spewing gravel.

The hot wind in her face stoked her frustration, and she pushed the bike's speed to seventy. She'd driven only two miles when she spotted a pickup parked on the shoulder of the road. Dollar signs flashed before her eyes. A stranded motorist needing a tow meant money in her pocket. She pulled off the road and scanned the area—a girl couldn't be too careful these days and she was too smart to walk into an ambush. Assured no one hid in the brush along the road, she turned off the bike and set the stand.

A movement caught her attention and she zeroed in on the pickup, where a pair of cowboy boots stuck out the driver's side window. She approached the vehicle cautiously and peered through the open window, finding a cowboy sprawled inside, his hat covering his face. Snoring sounds echoed through the cab—whether he was sleeping off a drink or resting while he waited for a ride was anybody's guess.

She slapped her hand against the bottom of one boot then jumped inside her skin when the man bolted into an upright position, knocking his forehead against the rearview mirror. His hat tumbled to the floor, and Destiny got her first good look at him.

Wow.

There was a hint of gold warmth in his brown eyes, the color reminding her of high-grade engine oil. Dark eyebrows stood out on a face framed by shaggy brown hair with sandy highlights. Without the cowboy hat he might easily be mistaken for a California beach bum.

Destiny wasn't used to running into sexy men—she lived in a town full of old people. "Need a lift?"

He glanced out the rear window. "Where's the groom?"

"If I knew the answer to that question, I wouldn't be talking to you right now."

He shoved his hand out the window. "Buck Cash." His deep baritone voice settled over her fringed vest like a soft caress. She shook his hand—thick calluses convinced her that he was the real McCoy, not some wannabe buckaroo.

"Destiny Saunders. Where are you headed?"

"Up to Flagstaff for a rodeo this weekend."

"What event?"

"You mind if I get out of the truck?" he asked.

She backed up. Then backed up again when he stood. The man towered over her five-foot-four frame. She eyed his broad shoulders and deep chest. "Tie-down roping?"

"I ride a bull every now and then." He settled his hat on his head, which added another two inches to his height.

"Where's your horse?" she asked.

"Don't own one. A buddy of mine loans me his when I compete."

This cowboy must only rodeo when he felt like it. "What's wrong with your truck?"

"Puncture in one of the hoses."

She doubted he'd even checked the engine. Ignoring his wide-eyed stare, she walked to the front of the truck. "Pop the hood."

He grinned—brilliant white teeth as straight as a ruler glinted in the sun. Self-consciously she ran her tongue over her crooked eyetooth. Once he released the latch, she secured the hood rod. "The cap looks fine."

He peered over her shoulder and she caught a whiff of musk-scented cologne. There wasn't a hint of wood or lavender or any other smell—it was pure raw male. A quiver that had nothing to do with the morning sickness she'd come down with a few days ago spread through her stomach. Steeling herself against the odd sensation she examined the engine.

"You've got a cracked hose." She stepped back and unhooked the rod then let the hood drop into place. "The nearest mechanic with a tow truck—" *her* "—is a few miles up the road in Lizard Gulch. You want a lift there?"

"If it's not too much trouble."

She waited by the Harley while he closed the truck windows and locked his gear inside the cab. "Guess you're going to miss your rodeo," she said.

"There's always another one." He eyed the bike. "This your motorcycle?"

"You think I ditched my fiancé at the altar and then took off on his bike?"

"Kind of looks that way." He kept a straight face but his eyes sparkled.

"Looks can be deceiving. Hop on." Once he was situated, she jumped on the kick-starter and gunned the engine.

His chest pressed into her back and sweat beaded between her breasts. She'd yet to come across a man who intimidated her, but there was something about the cowboy that put her off-balance. "Where should I hold on?"

"Wherever you want." She checked the mirrors then shot onto the highway. Once the tires gained traction, she shifted gears. When the hog jumped forward, his hands clasped her hips, his fingers squeezing until she felt the pressure against the bone.

Her driving made him nervous. *Good.*

She hit a straightaway and the hog's speed edged toward eighty. She knew the road like the back of her hand—every pothole, bump and crack in the asphalt—and had complete control of the bike. The first time she'd given Daryl a ride on the Harley, he hadn't been half as nervous as the cowboy.

Speaking of Daryl... Funny how she'd forgotten the father of her baby the moment Buck had stepped from the truck. Maybe things had worked out for the best when Daryl had chickened out at the eleventh hour. Had they tied the knot, they'd probably have been divorced inside of a year.

BUCK FELT LIKE an extra in a Hollywood movie. He'd woken this morning ready to rodeo and now here he was, hitching a ride on a Harley with a runaway bride. He swatted the lace veil away from his face. Life sure had gotten interesting since his older brother Will had all but kicked him off the family pecan farm and told him to get the heck out of Dodge for a while. Buck was the first to admit he'd deserved the banishment.

Will had learned for the first time this past June that he had a fourteen-year-old son. The mother had been a girl he'd taken to the prom his senior year. After Marsha Bugler graduated high school, she'd left Arizona to attend college in California. Buck had kept in touch with her through email and then one afternoon a year ago in March he'd surprised Marsha with a visit on the way home from a rodeo and had met her son for the first time—a teenager who'd looked suspiciously like Will.

Marsha had confessed that Will was the boy's father, then begged Buck not to tell him until she figured out the best way to break the news. He'd agreed to keep Marsha's secret, believing she'd follow through on her promise. A month passed then another and another, and it wasn't until a year and a half later that she wrote Will a letter, informing him that he was a father. Buck didn't blame his brother for kicking him to the curb, and he'd left willingly while Marsha and Will sorted through the wreckage of their past and figured out their future as a family.

Once in a while Buck checked in with his younger sister Dixie, but he never told her his whereabouts. Since leaving home in June, his brother Johnny and his wife, Shannon, had delivered a baby girl, named Addy in honor of Grandma Cash. And just last week

Dixie had texted him the news that Will and Marsha had married.

Almost daily Dixie begged Buck to come home, but he wasn't ready. He couldn't say for sure what kept him away from Stagecoach. He only knew that he didn't want to go back to the same-old-same-old—a rodeo once a month and working on cars in Troy Winters's garage. His brothers were moving on with their lives, and he wanted to move on, also—to where and to what was anyone's guess.

The road curved and Destiny slowed the bike. Buck relaxed his grip on her slender hips as the faint scent of lilacs drifted up his nostrils. He didn't know if the scent came from her skin or the red locks she'd pinned to the top of her head. He dropped his gaze to the bare shoulder in front of him. Crawling out from the edge of the sleeveless vest was a red, yellow and green lizard, its tongue extended toward a tiny tattooed fly. Despite her petite size, Destiny was solid muscle. Maybe she was a personal trainer at a fitness gym—that would explain her toned arms.

One more mile and the bike slowed to a crawl then veered onto a dirt road badly in need of grading. It wasn't until the bike crested a small mesa that he spotted the handful of buildings in the middle of the desert. Twin palm trees stood a hundred feet in the air above the buildings and looked out of place in the dusty barren landscape.

His escort coasted into town—if the place even qualified as a town. He counted six structures. The towering palms guarded the entrance to the Flamingo Inn Resort—a seen-better-days motel that had been converted into a trailer park. A gas station with one repair bay and one pump sat at the end of—he read the street sign—Gulch Road. Carter Towing and Repair had been painted in red block lettering across the front of the whitewashed brick.

The Florence Pastry Shoppe, a two-story Victorian-style home, faced the motel on the opposite side of the street. A giant-sized croissant twirled atop a pole mounted to the roof. Three white rockers sat on the front porch.

Instead of driving to the garage, Destiny parked outside Lucille's Smokehouse Grill and Saloon, which sat next to Dino-Land, a nine-hole miniature golf course whose entrance was guarded by giant plaster dinosaurs, their green paint faded and cracked.

She cut the bike engine and Buck heard the faint sounds of piano music. "What's going on?"

"My wedding reception."

Uh-oh. Even though Destiny didn't act upset, he doubted the jilted bride looked forward to informing her wedding guests there was nothing to celebrate. He caught her arm when she stepped past him. "If you want, I'll tell them the wedding was called off."

For the first time since they'd met, she removed her sunglasses. Buck sucked in a quiet breath as he felt himself being dragged into the undertow of Caribbean blue waters. The eyes staring up at him were perfectly round and easily the largest feature on her freckled face. "Thanks, but it's not a big deal."

Not a big deal? What kind of man had she been engaged to? She climbed the steps to the saloon and he couldn't help but notice that the white leather pants fit her firm little fanny like a glove. The groom had a screw loose if he let a woman like this get away.

"You're welcome to come inside for food and drinks," she said.

The other businesses appeared deserted. The entire population of Lizard Gulch, including the mechanic, Buck guessed, waited inside the bar.

"What's it gonna be?" She tapped her boot heel against the wooden boardwalk. He took the steps two at a time then held the door open for her. As soon as she entered, the piano music switched to "Here Comes the Bride." A group of geriatrics stared—mouths hanging open, their gazes swinging back and forth between Destiny and Buck.

A barrel-chested man who wore his long gray hair in a ponytail eyed Buck suspiciously before speaking to Destiny. "I thought you were marrying Daryl? Where'd you find this guy?"

"He's a whole lot better-looking than Daryl." A skinny man with gray sideburns and a receding hairline patted his chest beneath his cobalt-blue silk shirt.

"This is…" Destiny sent Buck a blank look.

Holy cow. She'd forgotten his name—that had never happened to him before. Not only was his moniker memorable, but most ladies thought his face was, too. "Buck Owens Cash."

"Buck Owens? Why Buck is one of my favorite country-and-western singers." A blonde lady wearing a strapless rhinestone dress that pushed her wrinkled bosom up to her chin batted her eyelashes.

"Heel, Sonja."

"Go soak your head in a bucket, Ralph," Sonja said.

"Whoever thought to name their kid Buck Owens Cash must have been a dimwit." A man closer in age to Buck moved to the front of the group. Dressed in a gray suit and red tie, he assessed Buck. "Is Cash your real surname or one you made up to go with your Vegas stage name?"

Stage name? "All three names are for real, and I doubt my deceased mother would appreciate you calling her a dimwit," Buck said.

"Knock it off, Mark. Buck's pickup broke down near the chapel and I gave him a lift into town," Destiny explained.

"You look very...hot." Sonja handed him a bottled water.

"Thank you, ma'am." Buck guzzled the drink.

"Where's Daryl?"

"What happened?"

"How come you're late?"

Questions were fired at Destiny from all directions, and she raised her hands in surrender. "Daryl was a no-show."

An elderly man with grizzled cheeks dressed in polyester slacks and a plaid dress shirt appeared at Destiny's side. He tapped his finger against what appeared to be a toy sheriff's badge pinned to his shirt. "Want me to bring him in?"

Was this guy for real?

"Thank you for your concern, everyone, but I'd rather Daryl have changed his mind about marrying me now than after we tied the knot."

The redhead didn't act the least bit heartbroken, which Buck found hard to accept. Then again a woman who sported a lizard tattoo and biceps muscles was probably as tough on the inside as she appeared on the outside.

"Violet." Destiny removed her veil and handed it to

a lady with blue hair. "I'm sorry I wasn't able to break the curse."

What curse?

"Never mind, dear," Violet said. "I shouldn't have loaned it out. I probably passed my bad luck on to you."

"Good Lord, Violet." A woman standing by the piano spoke. "That wedding veil has made a dozen trips down the aisle and not one of those marriages lasted more than a few years."

"Eleven, and none of the divorces were my fault." Violet winked at Buck. "Can't help it if I'm attracted to bad boys."

Buck felt his face heat up.

Destiny came to his rescue. "No need to let all this food and drink go to waste."

"We never celebrated Destiny's mayoral win," the sheriff said. "We should turn this into a victory party."

The biker chick was the mayor of Lizard Gulch?

"Three cheers for Destiny!"

Hoots and hollers echoed through the bar then folks crowded the buffet table, loading their Chinet plates with every kind of casserole known to mankind.

Someone pushed him toward the food line. "Go eat."

He did as he was told, then stood in the corner and watched Destiny make the rounds, chatting with her constituents and listening to their complaints and concerns as if she really cared.

"Is this your first time in Lizard Gulch?" Mr. Suit-and-Tie held out his hand. "Mark Mitchell."

After he shook Mitchell's hand, Buck said, "Until a few minutes ago I wasn't aware the town existed."

"Lizard Gulch used to be a lively place in its day."

"And when was that?" *A century ago?*

"Five decades of prosperity before the Interstate took all the traffic north of the town. Lizard Gulch was a popular overnight stop on the old Route 66." He pointed to a lady a few feet away, whose shoulder-length black bob looked like a wig. "Melba's parents ran the Flamingo Resort. Travelers stopped here on their way to California, because the motel had an outdoor pool and slide for kids." Mitchell wiped his brow with a napkin. "Once they finished construction of the Interstate, people drove straight through to California."

"I'm surprised the town wasn't abandoned." How did anyone make a living? Then again, the average age in the saloon had to be sixtysomething. Maybe they were all retired.

"The town sat vacant for years. When Melba's husband died, she quit her job as a bank teller in Kingman, then took his insurance money and renovated the Flamingo. Turned the parking lot into a mobile home park and invited friends to visit. Her friends told their friends and before you knew it the place filled up with old farts."

Buck eyed the bride. Why would a young woman want to live with all these gray heads? "How long has Destiny lived here?"

"About a year."

"Stop hogging the newcomer." The guy wearing the disco shirt slipped his arm through Buck's and squeezed his biceps. "We haven't had a cowboy as handsome as you come through town in...*forever*."

"Enrick's one of those homosexuals, but you probably already figured that out," Mitchell said.

Buck choked on a swallow of water.

"It's called being gay, Mark." Enrick motioned to

the big man with the ponytail. "Frank's my partner. We met at a pastry competition in Phoenix and it was love at first sight."

Buck barely heard Enrick drone on about his partner— Destiny had caught his attention. She'd taken the pins out of her hair and long fiery locks cascaded down the back of her white leather vest. She was nothing like the women he normally dated. Maybe that weekend rodeo in Flagstaff wasn't so important after all.

"Where are you from?" Mitchell asked.

"Stagecoach. Small town southeast of Yuma."

Enrick leaned in and sniffed Buck's neck. "You smell good. What cologne are you wearing?"

Buck inched sideways, inserting an extra foot of space between himself and lover boy. "I can't remember."

"I've never cheated on Frank—" Enrick sighed dramatically "—but right now I really wish I was single."

Frank made his way through the crowd toward Enrick and Buck. "Quit pestering the guest," he said as he turned Enrick toward the buffet table. "Go eat. You're too skinny."

"I just love how you worry about me." Enrich stood on tiptoe and kissed Frank's cheek then was off to join a group of gossiping women.

"Sorry about that," Frank said. "He comes on a bit strong."

No kidding.

"You're not gay, but watch yourself with Enrick. He has a way of making a man think twice about his sexuality." Frank walked off, leaving Buck shaking his head not knowing what to think.

The sheriff wheeled a cart carrying a wedding cake

across the floor and everyone oohed and ahhed over the green frosting lizards crawling up the white monstrosity. A plastic bride and groom riding a motorcycle sat on the top tier.

"This is beautiful, Frank." Destiny hugged the pastry chef.

"The lizards were my idea." Enrick beamed.

Frank wielded the knife. "Who wants a piece?"

After all the guests were served, Destiny brought Buck a slice. "Wild bunch, aren't they?" She smiled fondly at the group.

He kept his opinion to himself and sampled the cake. "Hey, this is good." When he finished the dessert, he asked, "Is the town mechanic here?"

"No."

"I'd better head to the garage and talk to him about my truck. Thanks again for the lift." Buck handed Destiny his empty cake plate then left the bar. As he walked down the middle of the street he noticed a cemetery tucked behind the miniature golf course. Three marked graves occupied the plot. A sign on the gate read Ghost Tours Daily at Dusk.

A shiver racked his body when he stopped and looked back at the saloon. The people in there hadn't been ghosts, had they? Shaking his head, he continued to the garage, wondering if he'd just landed in *The Twilight Zone*.

Chapter Two

Destiny braced herself when Mark Mitchell, the *former* mayor of Lizard Gulch, approached her. The sleazy lawyer found satisfaction in others' misery and she'd love to slap that condescending grin off his face.

"So…I wonder why Daryl didn't show up at the chapel?"

"I guess he decided he didn't love me enough to marry me." Too bad she wasn't heartbroken over being jilted.

"You know," Mitchell said, "if there were opportunities to make a decent living in this town, he might have taken a chance on you."

Money had never been an issue between her and Daryl. He did his thing and she did hers. When they could coordinate their schedules they hung out together.

"There's time to win Daryl back. All you have to do is convince your constituents to take the deal Wyndell Resorts is offering." Mitchell's grin widened. "Once you have all that money in your pretty little hands, your fiancé will come running back."

Mitchell had arrived in town a year ago, claiming he was searching for a place to retire. She hadn't bought the lie—a man in his late thirties was too young to be thinking about retirement, but he'd sweet-talked the residents into believing he was a nice guy before he'd convinced them that the town needed a mayor. Of course he'd insisted he was the man for the job. The five-member town council swore him in as mayor and thirty days later Mitchell presented a proposal from a land developer who wanted to buy the town and replace it with a resort and golf course.

The issue divided the town—half wanted to sell, the other half insisted the developer shove his proposal where the sun didn't shine. Destiny sided with the *shovers*.

"What if I don't want Daryl back?" She sipped her water.

"Think of all the things you could buy with the money Jack Custer is offering."

Even though the town was torn over the buyout offer, the residents had all agreed that Mitchell had misrepresented himself. The council recalled him as mayor then selected Destiny to replace him. The very next day she'd driven to Phoenix and had met with Wyndell Properties. Custer had treated her like a petulant child, sending her back to Lizard Gulch with a new offer to present to everyone.

When Destiny explained Custer's proposal—a $75,000 per person payout—those in favor of saving the town snubbed their noses at the money and those in favor of selling wanted to sign on the dotted line right then and there.

The town was at an impasse with Destiny caught in the middle. As mayor she represented every resident, but she hated to see the buildings bulldozed. The residents had welcomed her with open arms and she considered all of them her family. That family would dissolve if Custer got his way.

Now that she was pregnant, it was more important than ever that she change the minds of those siding with Wyndell Resorts. She refused to raise her child the way she'd been brought up—traveling from one place to the next. Living in public restrooms and truck stops. Eating in soup kitchens. Destiny had never attended school. Waitresses at various truck stops had taught her to read and write, and after she'd run away and the Carters had become her foster parents, Sylvia Carter had homeschooled her. Eventually, she'd earned her GED—an accomplishment she was very proud of. Yet a GED did little to help her fight off bullies like Mark Mitchell and Jack Custer.

"You know," Mitchell said. "Maybe Daryl got a better offer from another girl?"

Destiny wouldn't put it past the lawyer to have paid her fiancé to ditch her at the church just because he was miffed she'd thrown a monkey wrench into his plans. She was well aware that Mitchell would earn a handsome bonus if he closed the deal between the land developer and the residents of Lizard Gulch.

"Don't be such a donkey butt, Mitchell." Melba slid her arm through Destiny's. "The poor girl's heart has just been broken."

"My heart will be fine." Destiny squeezed the older woman's veiny hand. If she had any remorse about Daryl's abandonment, it was for their baby. Her mother had never talked about Destiny's father and always brushed aside her questions about him, suggesting she hadn't known which of her customers had fathered her child. Whether or not Daryl chose to be involved in their baby's life was up to him, but she'd make sure her son or daughter knew who his or her father was.

"I think Violet's looking for you, Mark," Melba said. After Mitchell walked off, she asked, "Where did that handsome cowboy go?"

Well, shoot. Destiny had forgotten that Buck Owens Cash was waiting at the garage. "I better leave. I need to fire up the wrecker and tow his pickup."

"You two stop in later," Melba said. "We'll be here all night."

Destiny slipped out the back door, walked past the cemetery and came up behind Carter Towing and Repair. She climbed the fire escape to the apartment above the garage and entered the one-bedroom dwelling. The place needed major renovations. She'd like to paint the walls, replace the linoleum flooring and install a shower in the bathroom, but with a baby on the way, her money would be better spent on a crib, car seat, diapers, clothes and a million other things.

In the bedroom she stripped to her skivvies and changed into her work jeans and her favorite Arizona Cardinals T-shirt. She secured her long hair in an elastic band then shoved her ponytail through the opening at the back of her Diamondbacks baseball cap. Lastly, she tugged on a pair of thick socks and stuffed her feet into her work boots. Simon Carter had taught Destiny the ins and outs of the towing business, including the importance of wearing steel-toed boots. Safety was her number one priority—even more so now that a child would be depending on her in seven months.

Truck keys in hand, she paused in front of the mirror to check her reflection—she'd never really cared what she looked like before. Why now? Maybe because Buck was unlike any guy she'd dated in the past.

For a girl who was supposed to get married today you've moved on pretty quick.

Destiny had no experience with boy-next-door types—they normally passed her over. But when Buck turned those warm brown eyes on her, she could almost believe that he saw something in her worth his time.

You're pregnant.

She cursed the voice in her head. She didn't need her subconscious to remind her that she was carrying another man's baby and that any guy in his right mind would steer clear of her. So be it, but she was entitled to her dreams, and it had been longer than she remembered since she'd fantasized about any man including Daryl.

She left the apartment and walked to the front of the building where Buck sat on the bench outside the office door. If only there was more than a broken hose wrong with his truck. She couldn't think of a better-looking distraction than the cowboy hanging around town for a few days.

As soon as he noticed her, he flashed his sexy white grin. Then his gaze roamed over her outfit and the smile vanished. "I thought you were celebrating your mayoral win?"

She shoved her fingers into the front pockets of her jeans. "They're celebrating without me."

"Do you know where—" he glanced at the side of the garage "—Mr. Carter is?"

"There is no Mr. Carter."

He removed his Stetson and ran his fingers through his shaggy hair. "I thought you said—"

"Simon Carter is deceased. I named the business after him."

"*You* named the business?"

Destiny spread her arms wide. "I run the garage."

His eyebrows arched.

"What?"

"You're the tow truck driver?"

"I'm also a decent mechanic."

Buck stared at Destiny, his mind trying to reconcile the redheaded biker bride with the tomboy standing before him in ragged jeans, a faded T-shirt and men's boots. In all the years he'd worked in Troy Winters's garage, not once had he run into a woman who knew car engines. Go figure the one time his truck breaks down a woman mechanic comes to his rescue.

"You don't believe me, do you?" she said.

"I've never met a lady mechanic before."

Her baby blues narrowed, as if she expected him to sling insults at her.

"How did you become interested in fixing cars?" he asked.

Tiny wrinkles formed across her tanned forehead. "Would you rather stand here and chat or do you want me to tow your truck?"

"Where do you plan to tow it?"

"Wherever you want. Kingman or…here."

He heard the hitch in her voice when she said the word *here*. Kingman was a safe bet—but maybe it was time he rolled the dice.

"If you've got replacement hoses in stock, it would be quicker to fix the truck here," he said.

Destiny paced a few feet away, leaving a trail of

scented perfume in her wake. "It'll be a hundred dollars for the tow and a hundred for parts and labor."

The sassy little mechanic wanted to rip him off. "That's highway robbery." Troy charged his customers twenty bucks for a new hose and fifty for labor, but he doubted Destiny got many customers this far out in the desert. He couldn't blame her for making the most of the opportunities that came her way.

"Have you ever had the hoses in your truck changed before?" She crossed her arms over her chest—she was cute when she got all feisty.

"No." He wanted to see how much she actually knew about engines. "This is the first time I've had a leaky hose." His gut tightened at the lie, but he kept a straight face. "Where's your wrecker?"

"This way."

He followed her behind the building then stopped dead in his tracks when he noticed the vehicle. Holy cow—the thing was a monster and in pristine condition. He watched Destiny climbed into the cab, admiring her athleticism as she hopped onto the running plate, took hold of the bar behind the driver's seat and hoisted herself into the cab.

He got in on the passenger side and shut the door. "What year is this?"

"It's a 2007 freightliner with a 12,000 pound integrated wheel lift, two 15,000 pound planetary winches and a Mercedes 250 HP engine." She quirked an eyebrow. "Any more questions?"

"This machine won't have a problem towing my Ford."

Like a pro, Destiny fired up the wrecker, shifted gear and drove onto Gulch Road.

"What's the deal with only three people buried in the cemetery?" he asked when the truck passed the burial ground.

"Melba says—"

"Who's Melba again?"

"She owns the Flamingo." Destiny waved at a man standing outside his mobile home next to the motel. "Back before Melba was born and her parents managed the property, there was a woman in town named Maisy Richards and she was engaged to a Victor Candor. Before the wedding took place, a stranger named Antonio Torres showed up in town and fell hard for Maisy."

"A love triangle," Buck said.

"Victor caught Antonio stealing a kiss from Maisy and threatened to kill him."

"Did Antonio go to the police?"

"No. Antonio waited for Victor to show up at his motel room and when he did, Antonio drew his gun and they shot each other dead."

"What happened to Maisy?"

"She hung herself from the tree that stands in the cemetery. Witnesses say she wanders through town after midnight calling for her lovers."

Buck laughed out loud. "That sounds made up."

Destiny shrugged.

"Have you heard Maisy call her beaus?"

"No, but there's rumors that people who stayed at the motel after the murders complained about hearing gunshots in the middle of the night."

"Interesting."

Destiny slowed the wrecker as she navigated a bend in the road.

Buck was amazed a woman her size handled the

truck with such confidence. He'd never met a female quite like Destiny—she was a puzzle he wouldn't mind solving.

"What's the matter?"

"Nothing," he said. "Just thinking."

"Has anyone ever told you that you look mad when you think?"

He relaxed his facial muscles. "I don't get how you can go from being left at the altar to towing my truck without missing a beat. Most girls would be bawling their eyes out and inconsolable."

"I'm not most girls."

That was for damn sure.

"I've had my share of disappointments and it began early in my life." Her fingers clenched the steering wheel. "Guess I've developed a thick skin." She slowed the wrecker when she passed the Ford then checked her mirrors and made a U-turn before merging onto the shoulder of the road in front of his truck. "This will only take a minute."

No way was he waiting in the cab. He had to see the pint-sized mechanic in action. "Can I help?"

"Sure."

"Tell me what to do."

"Stay out of my way." She lowered the boom arm in the back of the wrecker then attached the wire cable from the tow winch to the front end of his pickup. In less than ten minutes she had his vehicle secured on the flatbed and ready to haul.

"I'm impressed." And he meant it. "Where did you learn to drive a wrecker?"

"Simon Carter. He showed up one night to tow an

abandoned car beneath an overpass in Phoenix and found me sleeping inside."

"How old were you?"

"Thirteen."

Holy smokes. "Why were you hiding in an abandoned car?"

Destiny started the engine, and after she pulled onto the road, she said, "I don't like to talk about my childhood."

"That makes two of us." His comment drew a sharp look from her, but she didn't prod him for details.

"Back to my original question, how—"

She glared at him.

"You don't have to tell me about your childhood. I just want to know how you ended up in a broken-down car beneath an overpass."

"I hitched a ride into Phoenix with a trucker and he dropped me off there. When Simon found me, he offered to call the police, but I refused, so he took me home with him and fed me."

"How old was Simon?"

"Sixty. Sylvia, his wife, is a sweet lady. She insisted I sleep in their guest bedroom. The next morning I expected social services to pick me up, but Simon and Sylvia said I could live with them until I figured out what my next move was."

"Generous people."

"Sylvia offered to homeschool me, and when I had free time I went out on calls with Simon in the wrecker." She shrugged. "After a few months they asked if they could adopt me and I said yes."

"How long did you live with the couple?" Buck asked.

"I was nineteen when Simon died of a heart attack."

Even though Destiny showed little emotion, he got the feeling Simon's death had affected her deeply. "I'm sorry."

"Sylvia sold the house and moved to Florida to live with her sister. She gave me Simon's truck, his tools and a little money. I advertised on Craigslist and made enough cash towing to pay for an apartment and keep gas in the truck."

"How did you end up in Lizard Gulch?"

"I'd been searching for a place to set down roots," she said.

"And when you ran across Lizard Gulch, the town shouted Home Sweet Home?"

"It's not such a bad place."

Buck had a hunch Destiny was looking for another Simon to replace the one she'd lost, and there were plenty of geezers in the desert hideaway to fill the role. "How do you get enough tows in this area to stay in business?"

"I answer calls for car accidents between here, Kingman and Flagstaff. I average about three tows per month."

"How many car repair jobs come along?"

"I'm lucky if I get one every sixty days and those usually come from referrals."

Destiny's towing business could bring in a lot more money in Tucson, Yuma or Phoenix. It didn't make sense for her to live in Lizard Gulch.

"Where are you from?" she asked.

"Ever heard of Stagecoach? It's southeast of Yuma."

"Sounds like another little town."

"It is. My six siblings and I grew up on my grandfather's pecan farm."

"You have six siblings?"

"Five brothers and one sister."

"Wow. You kept your mother busy."

"Not really. Our grandparents raised us." He guessed he and Destiny had that in common—depending on old people.

"So you chose rodeo instead of farming?"

"My brother Conway manages the pecan orchard. He and his wife and their twin sons moved into our grandparents' house. My eldest brother, Johnny, recently married and had a daughter."

"You're kidding, right?"

"Kidding about what?" he asked.

"Your brother…*Johnny Cash?*"

Buck grinned. "My mother named my brothers and me after country-and-western legends."

Destiny grinned. "Tell me the names."

"I'm glad we amuse you."

"C'mon…"

"In order of birth," he said. "Johnny Cash, Willie Nelson Cash, me, Merle Haggard Cash, Conway Twitty Cash and Porter Wagoner Cash."

"Wow. You guys must have taken a beating on the playground with those names."

"I've had plenty experience defending my moniker." He smiled grimly. "Johnny and his wife live on his father-in-law's ranch, where he's the foreman. Earlier this summer Will married the woman he got pregnant in high school and met his fourteen-year-old son for the first time."

"She kept their baby a secret from your brother?" Destiny's shock appeared genuine. "That's not nice. Your brother had a right to know he was a father."

Destiny's statement made Buck feel all the more guilty that he hadn't told Will right away about Ryan when he'd found out the truth.

"But I guess he forgave her and they worked things out if they got married," Destiny said.

"They did. I didn't go to the wedding."

"Why not?"

"It's complicated," he said.

"You said you have a sister?"

"Dixie. She's married and had a baby boy named Nathan. She's a businesswoman like yourself. Runs a gift shop in Yuma and sells soap."

"What kind of soap?"

"Fancy girl stuff. My grandmother's relatives were soap makers in France, and Dixie uses the family recipes for her homemade suds."

"Cool."

Buck felt bad talking about his family when Destiny didn't have one of her own. "Do you keep in touch with Sylvia?"

"We call each other once in a while and she sends me a keepsake of Simon's every now and then. This past Christmas she gave me his military flag."

"They never had any children of their own?" he asked.

"No. Are you real close to all your brothers?"

"I guess." Then he'd gone and screwed things up with Will, and now they weren't talking.

When they arrived in Lizard Gulch, Buck noticed the lights were on in the saloon. "The reception hasn't died down."

"Old people never sleep. They'll party until they run out of liquor."

She backed his Ford into the repair bay like a pro then hopped out and released the lift. While Buck waited inside the garage for her to park the wrecker behind the building, he examined the collection of auto parts stored on a utility shelf. She had three boxes of hoses and it took thirty minutes to swap out a hose. He'd be back on the road in an hour.

"There's a chair in the office if you want to wait in there. The TV remote is on the counter."

He'd rather watch Destiny change his hose. He went into the office and switched on the TV. After fifteen minutes he lost interest in the home improvement show and returned to the bay. Destiny lay on a creeper beneath his truck. "Almost finished?"

The clanking sounds stopped, and she rolled into the open then got to her feet. She avoided making eye contact with him. "You've got a bigger problem than a ruptured hose."

"What are you talking about?"

"You must have driven over some debris, because the axel is broken."

"What?"

Destiny wiped her hands on a rag. "I don't have a spare axel. I'll have to order one."

"How long will that take?"

"A few days. Maybe a week."

"I'm stuck here until my truck is fixed?"

She nodded.

"Where am I supposed to stay? The Flamingo isn't even a motel."

"Melba has one room she rents to guests."

"How much does she charge?"

"Fifty dollars a night," Destiny said.

This was becoming one hell of an expensive breakdown. "I guess I'm staying."

"I'll order the part now." Destiny went into the office and shut the door.

Buck dropped onto the creeper and rolled himself beneath the truck. Sure enough. The damn axel hung crooked. He couldn't remember hitting anything on the road. He examined the break.

Well...well...well... The axel wasn't broken, it had been loosened.

Destiny had stranded Buck in Lizard Gulch on purpose.

Chapter Three

"What are you doing under there?" Destiny's voice echoed through the garage.

Buck used his feet to move the creeper out from beneath his truck. "I wanted to see the damage." He studied her face, but her nonchalant expression gave nothing away. She didn't come across as the kind of girl who'd swindle others, but maybe she was in a bind and needed money.

"I ordered a new axel. It should get here in three to five days," she said.

Kingman was an hour west of Lizard Gulch. She could drive into town tomorrow, buy the part and install it by noon, then he'd be on his way. Buck considered calling her bluff—mostly because he didn't want her to believe he was a dunce she could easily dupe—but he held his tongue. He wanted to find out what her game was.

The jilted biker bride with tattoos was a tough cookie, yet whenever she made eye contact with him the vulnerability in her blue gaze tugged at his heart, which confused the hell out of him because she wasn't his type. He was attracted to the girl-next-door, who in his experience had always been reliable, dedicated and loyal—

the exact opposite of his mother, who'd abandoned her children on and off through the years while she chased after her next true love.

"Not much to do in town while I wait for the truck to get fixed." He scrambled to his feet.

"The Lizard Gulch annual pool party at the Flamingo is tomorrow." She scuffed the toe of her work boot against the cement floor.

Buck decided to give her one more chance to come clean with him. "Are you sure the axel isn't just loose?"

"You're a cowboy not a mechanic." Her chin jutted. "I know what I'm doing."

He didn't doubt that for a minute. "I'll head over to the motel and see about renting a room." Neither of them moved, and he swore tiny heat waves wiggled in the air between them. His cell phone beeped with a text message, breaking the spell. "See you tomorrow." He'd look forward to viewing Destiny in a bikini and discovering if she had more tattoos on her sexy little body.

"Good night." She went into her office and shut the door behind her.

Buck left the garage and walked down the street. When he passed Lucille's Smokehouse, the self-appointed sheriff of Lizard Gulch stepped outside.

"Hey, Bernie," Buck said.

"You get your truck repaired?"

Buck stopped. Destiny's Harley still sat parked in front of the bar. "Broken axel."

"Sounds expensive."

"Destiny had to order a new axel, so I'll be in town for a few days." He motioned to the Flamingo. "I was on my way to see about renting a room."

"Melba's in the bar. Wait here." Bernie disappeared inside then a minute later the motel owner appeared.

"Bernie said you need a place to stay while your truck's being fixed."

"Destiny said you might have a room to rent."

"C'mon." Melba sashayed across the road, the strands of her black wig swinging back and forth across her face. She entered the lobby, and Buck swore he'd stepped into the late 1950s.

"Most people get that look on their face when they come in here," she said. "My mother put her heart and soul into decorating this place, and I haven't changed a thing since I took over."

Green carpet with tiny pink flamingos woven into the design covered the floor. A pair of white bubble chairs sat in a corner next to a modern olive-colored sofa and rectangle coffee table with stick legs on which a large chrome pelican ashtray rested. And there was a no smoking sign above the couch next to a mirror made of overlapping circles.

A vintage solid-state radio took up half the space on the pink laminate check-in counter. A starburst chrome clock that had stopped ticking at three-fifteen who knows how many years ago was mounted to the wall next to the desk. And above his head a large chrome Sputnik chandelier hung from the ceiling. Buck opened the guest register and perused the names and dates of past motel guests, noting George and Mildred Hunter from Saint Louis, Missouri, had been the motel's first customers and had stayed the night of September 5, 1953. The last guest to sign the book had been How-ard Nicholson June 12, 2013. Melba held out a pink flamingo-shaped pen. Buck scribbled his name and the date.

"Mr. Nicholson was a reporter for a travel magazine called *Out West*," Melba said. "He wanted to include the Flamingo in a feature story covering Route 66 motels." She reached beneath the counter and selected a pink bath towel, washcloth, bar of soap in the shape of a flamingo and small bottle of shampoo. "If you need anything else, let me know."

"You wouldn't happen to have a razor, would you?"

"I'll check." She left the lobby through a back door and reappeared a few minutes later with a lady's pink disposable razor.

"Thanks," he said.

She walked out from behind the counter and went to the lobby door.

"Don't you want my credit card number?" he asked.

She waved him off. "We'll settle the bill when you leave."

Trusting woman. He followed Melba along the walkway to the last door. "This is the only room I rent to guests."

"What about all the other doors we passed?" Buck had counted seven.

"I knocked down the walls between those rooms and made the space my private living quarters."

"Wait a minute." Buck blocked Melba's hand before she slid the key into the lock. "Is this the room where Victor and Antonio died?"

"How'd you hear about that?"

"Destiny told me the story behind the people buried in the cemetery."

"Don't worry." Melba opened the door. "The blood

was cleaned up years ago and my parents replaced the carpet and repainted the walls."

Buck entered, wondering if he was about to embark on a Caribbean adventure. The room had a floor lamp in the shape of a palm tree, flamingo bedspread and matching curtains, bamboo headboard and nightstand and the same green-and-pink flamingo carpet that was in the lobby. He peeked behind the bathroom door—a pink shell-shaped sink, pink toilet and tub with pink-and-white tile.

Melba turned on the air-conditioning unit beneath the window. "If you keep the room at eighty, I'll give you a break on your bill when you check out."

Eighty? "Sure," he said.

"Lucille's is the only place that serves food in town— unless you just want to eat pastries." She went to the door. "The Lizard Gulch pool party and barbecue kicks off at four tomorrow."

"Destiny mentioned the party. Where's the pool?"

"Behind the motel."

"I'll be there." He had nothing better to do while he waited to see what Destiny was up to.

After Melba left, Buck stared at the flamingo bedspread, wondering how many people had slept beneath the cover or if it had ever been dry-cleaned in the past two decades. His phone jingled, reminding him that he hadn't answered the text his sister had sent earlier.

Guess what? Marsha's teaching physics at the Yuma Junior College and Ryan got accepted into the accelerated program at the high school. Come home. We miss you.

Even though things had worked out between Will and Marsha, that didn't mean his brother was ready to forgive Buck.

He texted back.

Thanks for the update. Hope little Nate is well.

Buck figured he had two brothers pissed at him now. Will, and Johnny after he'd missed the birth of Johnny's daughter Addy in June. He left the room and headed back to the garage to fetch his rodeo gear and duffel bag.

One of these days he had to go home—whether he was ready or not.

DESTINY REMOVED HER dinner from the microwave and sat outside on the stoop to eat. From her vantage point above the garage she had a great view of the town and the Flamingo Motel at the opposite end of Gulch Road. Her gaze zeroed in on the room farthest from the main office, and she imagined Buck moving around inside. Was he taking a shower? Or resting on the bed watching TV?

What in the world had gotten into her—loosening the axel on Buck's truck? Maybe Daryl ditching her at the altar bothered her more than she cared to admit. *No.* She honestly believed he'd done them both a favor by not showing up at the chapel. He'd yet to respond to any of her calls. He might not have his act together, but he wasn't heartless and eventually he'd show up in town with an apology.

Daryl was the least of her worries. Without health insurance, finding care for her and the baby had been difficult. At least she'd located a women's clinic in

Kingman that had charged her next to nothing for her first prenatal appointment. Afterward, they'd sent her on her way with a free bottle of prenatal vitamins and several pamphlets on nutrition and the stages of the baby's development, which she was instructed to read before her next appointment.

A movement out of the corner of her eye caught her attention, and she squinted into the darkness. The door at the end of the motel opened and Buck emerged. When she'd come across his truck on the side of the road, she'd suddenly forgotten about Daryl, the baby she carried and the town's problems. And then he'd smiled and her heart had stumbled.

Buck walked across the street to Lucille's—he probably needed a drink. The first thing she'd learned when she'd moved to this town was that there was never a shortage of alcohol. According to the residents, whiskey cured hundreds of old-age ailments.

Destiny finished her dinner then showered before settling into bed and reading *Pride and Prejudice* by Jane Austen. Melba had loaned her the book, insisting Austen was a highly acclaimed author. Destiny didn't understand the book at all or any of the behaviors of the Bennett sisters. If it had been left up to her, she'd have told both Mr. Darcy and Mr. Bingley to kiss her ass then she'd have left town and struck out on her own.

A banging sound in the garage below the apartment interrupted her reading, and she bolted to the window. Buck left the repair bay, his duffel bag in one hand and his saddle propped on his shoulder. She watched him make his way back to the motel, wishing she could go with him.

She wasn't the kind of girl most boys took home to meet their mothers, and she wasn't a saint—she'd spent a night or two in motel rooms with men she shouldn't have—but Buck made her yearn to experience the teenage milestones she'd missed out on. Like a girl's first crush—that moment when she saw the guy of her dreams and her breath froze in her lungs. And a girl's first kiss—hers had been from a drunk who'd mistaken her for her mother in the truck stop restroom.

Men had come and gone from her life but never once had any of them, including Daryl, made her yearn for more than what was right in front of her.

She and Daryl had been friends who'd ended up in bed together one night. Even though Daryl had made her feel less alone in the world, hours would pass by when he wouldn't cross her mind. Unlike Buck, who'd been in her every other thought since she'd first come upon him sprawled inside his truck.

You don't even know if Buck has a girlfriend or if he's married.

The cowboy wasn't wearing a wedding band but that didn't mean squat. This was all foolishness on her part. Whimsy. She'd be better off reading thrillers than filling her mind with fantasy.

Tomorrow she'd tighten the axel on Buck's pickup and replace the hose then send him on his way—after the pool party.

Seeing the cowboy without a shirt on would provide her with a lasting memory after he left Lizard Gulch in the dust. To hell with Mr. Darcy and Mr. Bingley—when she went to sleep at night she'd conjure up an image of Buck and drift off to dreamland.

Buck wasn't sure what to make of the pool party. An assortment of old women wearing flowered swim caps played in the water surrounded by floating toys and chairs, while the other guests drank margaritas in red Solo cups with tiny umbrellas and flamingo stir sticks. A table in the shade held the leftover casseroles from Destiny's wedding/mayoral reception the night before, and bottles of beer and water sat on ice in a rusted-out horse trough.

"The cowboy's here!" Bernie waved from his inflatable dolphin chair floating inside a circle of heads covered with bathing caps. He'd pinned his sheriff's badge to the front of his John Deere cap and wore a camouflage T-shirt and matching swim trunks along with white tube socks—the old man must be worried about getting his feet sunburned.

Buck searched the AARP crowd but didn't spot Destiny.

"She'll be here soon." Melba stopped at his side. The twinkle in her eye suggested that she was aware of Buck's interest in the mayor. "I imagine she's catching up on sleep after going on a call at 3:00 a.m."

He didn't like the idea of Destiny alone on a deserted road late at night. There were too many weirdos out during those hours.

"The highway patrol asked her to pick up an abandoned car," Melba said.

"I didn't hear the wrecker." Buck should have heard the tow truck since the town dead-ended at the garage and the only road in and out sat twenty yards from his motel-room door.

"When you get to be my age, you don't sleep much. I was reading my gossip magazine in the lobby when she drove past. I called her, and she told me where she was going."

So Melba played the role of mother hen as well as motel manager. She stared at his body. "Don't you own a pair of swim trunks?"

He chuckled. "I knew I'd forgotten something when I packed for the rodeo."

"I can help."

Inside the motel office Melba set a cardboard box filled with mismatched clothing on the counter. "This stuff was left behind by guests. Maybe there's a swimsuit that'll fit you." She left, and Buck rummaged through the clothing, finding a pair of blue trunks with giant yellow pineapples on them. "These might work." No sense changing in his room. He stepped behind the counter and removed his jeans then yanked on the trunks. The suit was a little snug but covered all the important parts. He'd left his sneakers on the floor of his truck so he searched for a pair of men's sandals or flip-flops but came up empty-handed. The thermometer hanging in the shade outside the office window read one hundred and two degrees—the asphalt parking lot would fry the soles of his feet if he walked to the pool barefoot.

He pulled his socks and boots back on, then tipped his Stetson over his forehead to block the sun, helped himself to a pink towel from the storage closet and left.

Wolf whistles greeted him when he returned to the pool. "Now that's a sexy look if I ever saw one." Enrick circled Buck, leering at his body. "Your ghostly legs and chest could use a little sun."

"Quit criticizing him," Frank said. "At least he's got a chest."

Enrick gasped. "What's wrong with my chest?"

The two lovers engaged in a spirited argument over their physiques with Bernie threatening to issue citations for disturbing the peace.

"I think the boots are sexy." Sonja shoved a margarita into Buck's hand. She wore sunglasses with lenses so big they made her look like a bug from outer space. "Tell me, Buck…is there a Mrs. Buck at home?"

"No, ma'am."

She squeezed his arm. "That's too bad, but I—"

"Sonja, leave the man alone." Ralph grabbed his wife's arm and escorted her to the other side of the pool, where a group of women sat in the shade.

"Eat," Melba said, nodding to the buffet table.

"I'm good right now, thanks." Buck had eaten a sandwich at Lucille's earlier in the afternoon while he'd listened to Hank's civil war stories. The bar owner's great-great grandfather had fought in the Battle of Picacho Peak northwest of Tucson, and the way Hank told the story his grandfather had been the last man left defending the mountain.

"C'mon," Melba said. "I'll introduce you to everyone."

Buck met the people who lived in the trailers next to the motel. Harriet and Bob Wilson from Bakersfield, California. Bob was a retired lineman, and Harriet had owned a beauty shop years ago. They didn't have any children. Another retired couple—Bud and Dorothy West—lived next to the Wilsons. Bud had been a welder and his wife a bookkeeper for a clothing store. They had one child, three grandchildren and five great grandchildren. Next he met Edith and Guy Heinrich, originally from Milwaukee, Wisconsin. Guy had owned a gas station before he'd retired. When Edith fell on the ice ten years ago and broke her hip, they'd packed their bags and drove south to retire in warmer weather. They had one child and four grandchildren.

After a while, Buck lost track of who was who and where they came from—his mind on Destiny, wondering why she'd settled among such an old crowd.

"Thought you'd be long gone by now." Mitchell appeared out of nowhere, wearing Bermuda shorts and a Tommy Bahama shirt. Melba excused herself to talk to one of her tenants about a problem with their septic.

"The axel on my truck was damaged. I'm stuck here longer than I planned," Buck said.

"While you're here maybe you can talk sense into Destiny."

"Talk sense into me about what?" Destiny stopped at Buck's side.

Wow. Buck's mouth dropped open. Destiny wore a black bikini with little white skulls and crossbones printed on the fabric. She'd pinned her long red hair to her head in a sloppy knot that begged for a man to stick his fingers in it and mess it up some more. His gaze roamed over her body, pausing on her breasts, where part of a tattoo peeked out from beneath the swimsuit top. As he stared down at all that sexiness crammed into a tiny body, he couldn't recall why he preferred taller women.

"Ms. Mayor," Mitchell said. Buck noticed the lawyer appeared oblivious to Destiny's hotness. *Idiot.* "Why don't you ask Buck to weigh in on the town's situation? A stranger's perspective might be helpful."

"Or better yet," Destiny said, "Maybe Buck can convince the *recalled* mayor to get the heck out of town and stay out?" Then she turned to Buck and said, "Take off your boots. You look ridiculous."

"Yes, ma'am." Buck sat in a lawn chair and removed his Ariats and socks then stood. When he noticed Destiny ogling his legs, he suddenly wished his trunks weren't so snug.

Mitchell stuck his fingers in his mouth and whistled. "I need everyone's attention." Once the Geritol crowd settled down, he said, "Jack Custer has put forth a new offer."

Destiny ground her back teeth together to keep from pushing Mitchell into the pool. Damn him for using the party—an event intended to bring the town together—as a means to divide the residents.

"How much is he willing to pay us this time?" Frank shouted above the rumblings.

"Wyndell Resorts is prepared to pay each resident of Lizard Gulch $80,000 for their property."

Destiny scoffed. "That's only $5,000 more than the previous offer."

"Eighty thousand dollars is a lot of money," a woman in a swim cap covered in daisies said. "I could use the cash to move my home down south to my daughter's property, and I'd have plenty left over to buy a new car."

"That's right," Mitchell said. "The money would improve everyone's standard of living."

"There ain't nothing wrong with my standard of living." Bernie paddled his dolphin across the water and clung to the edge of the pool next to where Mitchell stood.

"What's going on?" Buck asked.

Destiny had hoped he wouldn't stick his nose into their business. The last thing she needed was a stranger swaying the town to take the developer's side. "A group of wealthy investors wants to buy Lizard Gulch, bulldoze the town and build a resort in its place."

"Lizard Gulch is in the middle of nowhere." Buck frowned at Mitchell.

"Ever see the movie *Field of Dreams?*" Mitchell asked.

"Build it and they will come?" Buck said. "That's what you're banking on?"

"Route 66 properties draw thousands of vacationers each year. Jack Custer studied this area and it's close enough to California that people will view an all-inclusive resort as a great weekend getaway."

"There wouldn't be much for resort guests to do if they don't play golf," Buck said.

Mitchell ignored Buck's comment and spoke to the group. "You've got one month to decide whether or not to take the new offer."

"What happens if we can't agree to sell or not?" Melba asked.

"You know that I consider you my friends," Mitchell said.

Destiny choked on her spit.

"When I was mayor I had to comply with state guidelines and submit answers to a questionnaire."

"What kind of questionnaire?" Destiny asked.

"I had to inform state officials that you haven't had the water well tested in fifteen years," Mitchell said.

"I've been drinking tap water for twenty years and I haven't gotten sick or died." Bernie cupped his hands in the water and directed a wave of it at Mitchell, who was forced to jump back to avoid getting his shorts wet.

"I also had to disclose to the state that none of you pay property taxes."

"Are you crazy?" Destiny spread her arms wide. "We don't pay taxes, because we don't use any fire or police services."

"And you have no place for children to go to school," Mitchell said.

The lawyer was grasping at straws. "Do you see any residents of child-bearing age?"

"Just you."

Destiny sucked in a quiet gasp. Had Daryl leaked that she was pregnant?

Mitchell raised his margarita glass. "A toast to becoming $80,000 richer."

"Destiny?"

Someone spoke her name then an arm curled around her waist, and the next thing she knew she was seated in a chair with Buck squatting in front of her. "You okay? You looked like you were about to faint."

"I'm a little thirsty."

Melba handed her a margarita.

"I'd rather have water, please."

Buck handed her a bottled water and filled a plate with chunks of watermelon and pineapple.

"Buck."

"Destiny."

They spoke at the same time. "You go first," she said.

"Is there anything I could do to help you at the garage while I wait on the new axel?"

"About that broken axel. There's something I need to tell you." She stopped short when Buck leaned forward, the golden glow in his brown eyes sending her pulse pounding through her veins.

"I could work on that car sitting in the back lot." He shrugged. "I don't know much about engines, but I could hand you tools."

His gaze dropped to her mouth, and all of a sudden Destiny forgot about being truthful with Buck. What could it hurt to wait another day before fixing the axel? "Have you ever changed the oil in your truck?"

"No, but I'm a fast learner."

The smile he flashed convinced Destiny that he was fast at a lot of things, the least of which was an oil change.

Chapter Four

"What happens if you don't get a majority of the towns-people to veto Wyndell Resorts' latest offer?" Buck was stretched out on a mechanic's creeper beneath Melba's 1990 black Pontiac Bonneville in the lot behind the garage. Destiny moved her creeper closer to him, the fresh scent of her perfume stirring his blood.

"Then we sell and Lizard Gulch will be wiped off the map." She held out her hand. "Give me the wrench."

Buck's fingers went straight for the tool Destiny asked for, then he remembered he wasn't supposed to know much about fixing cars. "Which one?"

Her gaze clashed with his. Their faces were only inches apart and he noticed her lashes were a dark brown. "Do you color your hair?" She frowned, and he said, "Most redheads have pale lashes."

"I don't dye my hair and the wrench I want is the one with a piece of yellow tape on it."

He handed her the tool and she loosened the large bolt. "Drip pan, please."

He held out the plastic container to collect the old oil.

"Thanks." She placed the pan on the ground, removed the cap and let the oil drain, then rolled out from beneath the car and stood. "The developer's offer stinks, and the land this town sits on is worth a lot more than $80,000 per person. Why else would Mitchell work so hard to convince everyone to pack their bags?"

Buck got to his feet. "I can picture the land being worth more once the resort is built but not now." He spread his arms wide. "There's nothing here that anybody would drive out of their way to see."

Destiny's head jerked as if he'd slapped her with an insult. "You may not think Lizard Gulch is special, but the people who live here do." She removed a rag from her pocket and wiped her hands hard enough to peel off a layer of skin.

"Guess it's a female thing—attaching emotional significance to a place."

"You mean you have no sentimental feelings about the pecan farm you grew up on?"

Sensing their conversation agitated Destiny, he sought to avoid an argument. "I have fond memories of chasing my brothers through the pecan groves, but when I think of home, its family that matters most—not the orchards."

Her expression softened. "When was the last time you were home?"

"A couple of months."

"Have you been riding the circuit all this time, or do you have a second place you use as a home base between rodeos?"

"Is that a polite way of asking if I have a lady friend I shack up with when I'm on the road?" He chuckled at the pink flush that spread across her cheeks. "I don't."

"What about when you're not on the road?" She looked him square in the eye.

Like wavy heat lines hovering over hot asphalt, sexual tension sizzled between them. This wasn't the first time he'd felt Destiny's attraction to him. Yesterday she hadn't taken her eyes off him at the pool party. And when he'd shown up at the garage earlier this morning, she'd stared at his mouth and licked her lips when he'd asked her how she'd slept the night before.

"I stay at the farm when I'm not rodeoing." He watched her carefully, but her neutral expression left him guessing at her thoughts. "May I ask you a question?"

"Sure."

"Is there a chance that you and Daryl might work things out?" If she had feelings for the runaway groom, Buck would call her out on the axel prank and leave Lizard Gulch sooner rather than later.

"No."

There hadn't been a flicker of doubt in her eyes when she'd answered him. "Positive?"

"Daryl and I never would have made it as a couple."

Now that he was confident Destiny was over Daryl, he wasn't sure what to do about his interest in her. He wasn't looking for a serious relationship. In truth, he didn't know what he wanted, except that he wasn't ready to go back to Stagecoach. "The oil has probably drained out by now."

His comment spurred her into action, and he watched with admiration as she added new oil to the engine and changed the air and cabin filters. "For a girl, you're good at car maintenance."

"How would you know?"

Caught in his own lie, he grinned. "I don't. You make everything look easy."

"I can teach you how to change the air filter," she said.

No thanks. "Do you have any other car work to do this afternoon?"

"This is it. Why?"

"Wanna go for a joyride in the desert?"

She laughed. "I'm guessing you want to test out my hog."

"I'd love to drive your bike."

"Have you ever handled a motorcycle before?"

"My brother owned a beat-up Harley in high school, and he let me use it on occasion."

"What kind of Harley?"

"I don't know. It was a lot smaller than the one you ride, and it sure didn't have a badass engine like yours has."

"Okay. I'll show you the boundaries of the town and where the developer wants to build the golf course." She carried the oil pan into the garage and Buck followed with the toolbox. "I need to change clothes," she said.

"You want a soda to take along?" He motioned to the vending machine in the office.

"I'll stick with water."

Buck fished coins from his pocket and bought a bottle of Gatorade instead of soda then looked over Destiny's hog.

"Think you can handle it?" she asked a few minutes later.

He nearly swallowed his tongue. She'd changed into a pair of cutoff jean shorts and a camouflage tank top that emphasized the shape and size of her breasts. The outfit was sexy, but paired with her black-heeled biker boots she looked like something straight out of a men's fantasy magazine.

"You're not worried about getting sunburned?"

He stared at her naked limbs, the skin sprinkled with freckles.

"I put on sunscreen." She gathered her long curls into a ponytail, then shoved a baseball cap on her head and spent the next five minutes giving him a crash course on motorcycle safety.

"You mind if I ask how much this bike cost?"

"It was a gift from Simon."

"The guy who took you in?" he asked.

"Yes."

"Pretty generous of him."

"Simon was like a grandfather to me."

Now that Buck was aware of the sentimental value of the bike, he'd make sure he took care driving it. "Do you have an extra helmet?"

"Do I look like a girl who uses a helmet?"

He grinned. "Let's get this party started."

Destiny placed a bottled water inside the bike compartment and Buck added his sports drink, then she stood back while he hopped on the jump start—the engine fired on the first try.

"Impressive." She climbed on behind him.

He waited for her to put her arms around his waist. Instead, she grabbed the handholds. Buck shifted gear and drove onto Gulch Road.

"Go out to the highway," she shouted in his ear as they passed the Flamingo.

Melba sat in the shade outside the motel office. She lifted her arm, making the sign for a trucker to blow his horn. Destiny reached past Buck and pressed the horn button. When he felt her breasts smash against his back, he gunned the engine and the hog shot forward. Destiny's fingers dug into Buck's waist, and she held on tight.

Payback sure was fun.

"THAT'S WHERE WYNDELL resorts plans to put the golf course." Destiny pointed north of where she and Buck stood on the shoulder of the road.

"They picked a scenic spot with the low-lying mountains to the south and the abandoned gold mine. Nice ambience for the golfers."

Destiny grudgingly agreed with Buck. "According to Mitchell, the entrance to the resort will be elevated so that when you're on the golf course you won't be able to see the highway, which—"

"Will make it feel like you're really out in the middle of nowhere," he said. "What about the hotel?"

"Behind the eighteenth tee."

"That means the guests won't see the highway, either."

"But they will see Lizard Gulch," she said. "The town will be visible from every window in the hotel which is why Custer wants to bulldoze the buildings."

"He should leave the town standing." Buck drank his Gatorade then said, "The buildings along with the old gold mine would lend the resort a nostalgic ambience."

"They're not going to touch the town." She kicked a rock, sending it flying through the air. When she glanced at Buck she caught him grinning. "What's so funny?"

"Nothing. I'm just…"

She perched her hands on her hips. "Spit it out."

"I'm awed by your…fighting spirit."

His compliment sucked the air from her lungs.

"You don't let anyone bully you, do you?"

"I'm not fighting because I love a good brawl," she said. "I'm trying to save this town, because it's more than a few buildings in the desert. It's a home to a group of people who've become my family. Selling Lizard Gulch would be like everyone divorcing and going their separate ways."

"You really care about those old people," he said.

"Someone has to look out for them."

Buck stepped forward and grasped her chin. "Who's going to look after you, Destiny?" Then he kissed her.

His kiss wasn't a gentle, getting-to-know-you caress but a full mouth-on-mouth-with-a-little-tongue embrace. He smelled like desert, faded cologne and warm man. Destiny relaxed in his arms, leaning against him as she threaded her fingers through his silky hair. Their tongues dueled, and she lost herself in the excitement and thrill of his touch.

The churning in her stomach went unnoticed until a sharp pain penetrated her aroused brain. Her fingers tightened against Buck's skull and she forced his head back, breaking off their kiss. Then she spun and vomited on a clump of wild Blackfoot daisies.

Buck held her by the shoulders and steadied her. "You okay?"

"I will be in a moment." How embarrassing. Of all the people she could have thrown up in front of, why did it have to be Buck?

"This is the first time one of my kisses has made a woman puke."

She laughed, her reaction triggering a second spasm, and she vomited again. Buck handed her the water she'd brought along, and his concerned expression melted her heart. She sipped, swished then spat. "Sorry you had to see that."

He took the bottle from her and doused his shirttail then dabbed at the moisture on her forehead and cheeks. "You sure you're okay?"

Destiny didn't answer right away—she was too caught up in a mini fantasy. Except for the fatherly concern Simon had shown her, she couldn't recall any man worrying about her well-being. Daryl hadn't even asked how she was feeling after she'd informed him she was pregnant.

"Destiny?" Buck rubbed the pad of his thumb across her cheek. "You didn't drink the leftover margaritas from the pool party for breakfast, did you?"

"No, but I think I caught a touch of food poisoning from the casseroles." Afraid to make eye contact for fear he'd read the truth in her gaze, she scuffed the toe of her boot against the ground.

"You should get out of the sun if you aren't feeling well." He walked beside her to the bike then placed his hand against the small of her back, steadying her as she swung a leg over the seat.

Feeling shaky, Destiny didn't think twice about leaning against Buck and wrapping her arms around him. He drove at an even pace back to town and she appreciated his effort to avoid the potholes in the road. When they pulled into the garage, he helped her off the bike but didn't release her hand. He peered at her face intently, his fingers rubbing her knuckles.

She wished he hadn't kissed her. When he'd held her in his arms, she'd felt safe from the big bad, ugly world. It was a feeling like none she'd experienced before—not even when the Carters had taken her into their home.

Sending him on his way would be more difficult than she'd anticipated.

Don't even think about keeping him here.

Not only was she pregnant with another man's baby, Destiny couldn't afford for Buck to stay in town long for fear she'd become accustomed to depending on him. And she'd learned the hard way from her mother and Daryl that the only person she could count on was herself. "Buck, there's something I need to tell you."

The despondent tone in Destiny's voice sent up a warning flag in Buck's head. Was she ready to come clean about the broken axel? Well, he wasn't ready to hear her confession—not after their kiss in the desert. "Go upstairs and rest. We'll talk later."

"But—"

He pressed his finger to her lips and swore he saw a spark in her blues eyes. There was definitely something happening between them, whether either of them was ready to admit it or not. She gave in and climbed the fire escape to the apartment above the garage. At the door she checked over her shoulder and the longing in her gaze stole the air from his lungs. Then she disappeared from view.

Buck had never been with a girl like Destiny—she was everything he'd never wanted in a woman—or he'd thought anyway. There was no denying the Harley princess made his motor race. He wanted—no *needed*—to take a walk on the wild side with her.

And let the chips fall where they may.

"How was your tour with Destiny?" Hank asked after Buck slid onto a barstool inside Lucille's.

"Good." Buck nodded to the beer taps. "I'll take whatever's on special today."

"It's Sunday. No alcohol on the Lord's Sabbath." Hank raised his arms in surrender. "I didn't make up the rule. The ladies temperance committee added the amendment to the town code last year."

"Temperance committee?" Buck didn't believe what he was hearing.

"The females outnumber us men. We didn't stand a chance when they put that law to vote." Hank leaned forward, resting his elbows on the bar. "That's why you don't see anyone outside. They're swiggin' medicine in their trailers. You'd be surprised at the physical ailments that flare up on Sundays."

"Guess I'll settle for a soda," Buck said.

Hank set the drink in front of Buck, then checked the clock on the wall. "It's almost noon. You hungry for a sandwich?"

"No, thanks." There wasn't an ATM in town to withdraw money and all he had left in his wallet was a hundred bucks.

The door opened and a gust of hot wind swept through the bar. A guy wearing baggy jeans and a T-shirt two sizes too big for his skinny frame walked in. He wore a buzz cut and was clean shaven, but tattoos covered both arms, the backs of his hands and his entire neck. "What's up," he said to Hank then sat three stools away from Buck.

"Daryl," Hank said.

Daryl? "You're the guy who left Destiny at the altar," Buck said.

The kid's eyes widened. "Who are you?"

"Buck's stuck in town until Destiny can repair the

broken axel on his truck." Hank slapped both his palms against the bar and glared at Daryl. "You got a good reason for not showing up to your own wedding?"

Daryl had the sense to look ashamed, making Buck believe the younger man wasn't cruel at heart—just uncertain or unsure.

Kind of like you.

Buck ignored the voice in his head.

"Rumors are floating through town that Mitchell paid you to stand Destiny up," Hank said.

That was news to Buck. "Is that the truth?" he asked. "Did Mitchell give you money to abandon your bride?"

Daryl squirmed on his stool. "He offered me a thousand dollars, but I wouldn't take it."

Buck didn't believe him.

"Destiny and I don't love each other." Daryl's gaze swung between the men. "Ask her. She'll tell you the same thing."

Hank grumbled then disappeared into the kitchen.

"Is that your truck sitting in the garage?" Daryl asked.

Buck refused to allow the kid to distract him. "If you don't love Destiny, why are you here?"

"We're still friends."

"Where did you two meet?" He eyed the serpent tattoo slithering down Daryl's arm.

"I'm a bouncer at a nightclub in Kingman."

What kind of nightclub employed skinny bouncers?

"Destiny came into the club to tell one of the dancers that she was towing her car and we got to talking and hit it off."

Daryl wasn't the kind of guy Buck pictured Destiny with. "Why are you here?"

Daryl scowled. "That's between me and Destiny."

Buck would prefer that Daryl leave town without seeing Destiny. "She's taking a nap right now." And just in case Daryl changed his mind about wanting more than friendship with her, Buck said, "We took a drive on her Harley today."

"She let you drive the Beastmaster?"

"Beastmaster?"

"She named her hog Beastmaster," Daryl said.

"I drove the bike."

"Lucky you. She never let me drive it."

That bit of news not only made Buck feel good but a little cocky, too. "You're right about Destiny," he said. "She's over you."

"How do you know?"

"We kissed this afternoon." Why was he acting like an adolescent jerk?

Daryl's skinny chest puffed up, but he didn't throw a punch, which told Buck better than words that the guy didn't have any deep romantic feelings for Destiny. "I better get going." Daryl stood. "I gotta be at work in a few hours."

Buck followed Daryl to the door then watched him cross the street and disappear behind the garage. He checked the clock, intending to keep track of how long lover boy stayed inside Destiny's apartment.

"Don't tell me you're jealous of that kid." Hank appeared at Buck's side.

"It's not like that between Destiny and me. Besides," Buck said, "I'm leaving at the end of the week."

"I'll believe it when I see it."

"What's that supposed to mean?" Buck asked.

"I caught you watching Destiny at the pool. You couldn't stop staring at her bosom."

"I was trying to figure out what that tattoo was beneath her swimsuit top." Buck ignored Hank's chuckle. "How old is Destiny anyway?"

"Twenty-three."

Buck would have guessed twenty-seven or twenty-eight. There was a world of experience and hard knocks in those pretty blue eyes of hers.

"There he is," Hank said.

Daryl walked around the side of the garage. Buck checked the clock on the wall. Ten minutes had passed—not enough time to have sex.

The saloon door opened and Daryl froze when he saw Hank and Buck at the window.

"You get things squared away with Destiny?" Hank asked.

"She's not mad."

"What happens between you two now?" Hank asked.

"Nothing." Daryl nodded at Buck. "She wants to see you."

Buck ignored the tiny jolt in his heart. When the kid reached for the door handle, he said, "Daryl."

"What?"

"If you ever hurt Destiny again, you'll have me to answer to." The words left Buck's mouth before he could stop them, and to tell the truth, he didn't know what the hell he meant by them.

Daryl slammed the door hard enough to rattle the saloon windows.

Hank grinned. "'Bout time that girl had someone in her corner."

Chapter Five

By late Wednesday afternoon, Buck was second-guessing his chivalry toward the cranky mechanic. Destiny had been as short-tempered as a woman wearing too-tight shoes. He didn't know if it was because she'd had zero tows the past forty-eight hours or because she was nervous about her meeting with the CEO of Wyndell Resorts.

After Destiny had given Buck a tour of the area on Sunday, she'd received a phone call from Custer and he'd invited her to Phoenix to meet with him and his staff. She'd refused, insisting that if the CEO had something to say he should talk directly to the residents of Lizard Gulch. Evidently the developer had never even stepped foot in the town. He'd sent Mitchell to do all his negotiating.

"Is the hotshot here?" Bernie entered Lucille's, the sheriff's star pinned to his T-shirt. He joined Buck at the bar.

"Custer's supposed to be here by five," Buck said.

Hank poured Bernie a glass of beer. "He'd better not be late."

"Why's that?" Buck asked.

"Wednesday night is bingo night."

What did one have to do with the other?

"The ladies will be spitting mad if bingo doesn't start on time," Bernie said.

As if on cue, the ladies of Lizard Gulch filed into the saloon—eleven of them, dressed in their Sunday best. Their husbands made a beeline for the bar.

"Myrtle's wearing that god-awful red dress with the matching feather hat and scarf again." Bernie chugged his beer. "Thought we'd decided someone should accidently set that outfit on fire."

"We did," Hank said, "but she locks her home up like Fort Knox and we can't get in to steal it."

Bernie tapped a finger against the plastic badge. "I'd be willing to look the other way if someone abducted Myrtle after bingo and demanded she strip out of her clothes."

Buck spun his stool to see this infamous red outfit for himself. The hat perched on Myrtle's head looked suspiciously like a bird's nest, and she wasn't the only woman in the crowd who resembled a feathered friend. Violet, the lady who'd loaned Destiny her wedding veil, could easily be mistaken for a canary in her teal-blue pantsuit, melon-colored blouse and yellow sneakers.

Ralph sauntered up to the bar. When he noticed the others staring at Myrtle, he said, "Sonja claims Myrtle shops at the Goodwill store in Kingman." He nodded his thanks when Hank set a beer in front of him. "You'd think by her age she'd have learned how to dress."

"You're the last person who should be mockin' Myrtle," Bernie said.

"Why's that?" Ralph's nostrils flared like a bull ready to charge.

"Your wife dresses like a hooker."

Buck choked on his water. These old men didn't pull any punches.

"You calling my wife a prostitute?" Ralph slid off his stool.

"Man's got a point," Hank said. "Those spandex pants Sonja wears don't leave a whole lot to the imagination… front or back."

Ralph jammed his elbow into Buck's side. "You got something to say about my wife's clothes?"

"No, sir," Buck said, even though he sided with the sheriff.

Melba waltzed into the bar and gave orders to push the tables together then she signaled Hank, who then disappeared into the back room and returned a minute later with a Las Vegas–style bubble top blower filled with white plastic balls. He set the machine on the table at the front of the room and plugged it in, while Melba handed out scorecards and Elvis and Betty Boop bingo markers.

"You gonna buy in tonight?" Bernie asked Buck.

"What do you mean buy in?"

"A dollar a bingo card. You gotta buy at least ten cards if you're gonna have a chance to beat Melba or Violet," Bernie said. "They're the bingo queens."

"I thought bingo was a lady's game," Buck said.

"What else is there to do in town on a Wednesday night?" Bernie squinted. "It's not like we can go down to the pier and fish."

Buck imagined his brothers' expressions if they discovered he'd played bingo with a bunch of old farts.

"Melba won three hundred dollars last month," Bernie said.

That wasn't small change.

While the ladies finished setting up the tables, Bernie droned on about chartered bus trips to Reno that the group had taken in the past. Buck was on the verge of excusing himself when the saloon door opened and Destiny walked in.

She wore a tight knee-length pencil skirt, a white silk blouse that showed a hint of cleavage and a matching suit jacket, which flared at the waist. His eyes zeroed in on her sexy tanned legs and trim ankles. She'd secured her red curls at the back of her head with a fancy clip, leaving a few wisps loose next to her face. This couldn't be the same woman who'd worn leather pants to her wedding, drove a Harley then threw on a pair of coveralls and got her hands dirty with engine grease.

"She's got her don't-mess-with-me getup on," Bernie whispered.

Right then, Mitchell entered the saloon, took one look at Destiny and stopped dead in his tracks. A slow smile spread across his face, and Buck's gut tightened with jealousy. He didn't like the way the former mayor leered at his girl.

Your girl? Buck ignored the voice in his head. Now wasn't the time to mentally debate his developing feelings for Destiny.

"Look," Bernie said. "Here comes Custer."

The door opened and the CEO joined the gathering.

"Listen up, everybody," Mitchell said. "This is Jack Custer, the CEO of Wyndell Resorts."

The tall man with jet-black hair and silver at the temples spread his arms wide. "It's a pleasure to finally meet the good citizens of Lizard Gulch." He grasped Melba's hand and kissed the back of it. The motel manager preened and batted her eyelashes. Then Custer walked through the bar, greeting the ladies and ignoring the men. When he stopped in front of Destiny, his expression sobered. "Hello, Ms. Saunders."

Destiny didn't offer her hand. "Whatever you came to say…say it. Bingo night kicks off in a few minutes."

Certain Destiny could handle Custer and Mitchell, Buck made himself comfortable on his stool and settled in for the showdown.

"Ms. Saunders, I'm here in person to officially present my offer to the townspeople."

Custer was doing his best to intimidate her, but Destiny refused to be cowed. Half the residents counted on her to defend the town, and the other half wanted her to get out of the way and allow the CEO to take over. Come hell or high water she'd prove to her constituents that Custer didn't have their best interests at heart.

"Mr. Custer has kindly agreed to meet with us and answer any questions you have about his plans for Lizard Gulch." Destiny made eye contact with each person in the bar. "I expect this gathering to remain orderly. Raise your hand if you'd like to speak. Mr. Custer won't leave town until every one of your questions has been answered to your satisfaction."

The first hand went into the air. "My name is Ralph Estevez and—" he pointed across the room "—that there's my wife, Sonja. We live rent free in Lizard Gulch." Ralph straightened his shoulders. "Your eighty thousand dollars ain't gonna go far. The average rent in a trailer park for two decades is a hundred-twenty grand."

Custer's laugh sounded like a bark. "I'm all for having a positive outlook but that's a stretch, believing the old ticker will work twenty years from now."

Destiny bristled and opened her mouth to demand Custer be more respectful, but Ralph wasn't finished speaking. "We're gonna suffer emotional stress if you force us out of our homes. Who's gonna pay for our shrinks?"

Custer's mouth dropped open, and Destiny covered her amusement behind a fake yawn.

"A fairer price for our land would be a hundred fifty thousand," Ralph said.

Sonja clapped her hands. "You tell him, Ralphie."

Custer's expression grew strained. "I understand your concerns and I'll consider compensating you for part of your moving expenses. As for any future psychiatric care—" he spread his arms wide "—wouldn't you be happier in a place where people like you—"

"People like us, what?" Bernie shouted.

"Retired people," Custer said. "There are several communities in Arizona that cater to couples in their twilight years." He motioned to the bingo machine. "There are lots of other activities—"

"You got something against bingo, Mr. Custer?" Melba asked.

"No, ma'am, but there's more to life than stamping cards."

Before a brawl erupted, Destiny raised her arm and the group quieted. She was aware Buck watched her every move, and part of her wanted to impress him— show him she had the upper hand with Custer and that she wasn't just playing at being the mayor. She didn't have a college degree, but she had plenty of street smarts and gut instinct insisted any offer the developer put on the table would only benefit him. "Mr. Custer, I think you need to explain how the payout works."

"After you send your paperwork to my lawyers—"

"What paperwork?" Hank spoke up behind the bar.

"The deed to your property," Custer said.

"Wait a minute." Bernie slid off his stool and approached Mitchell. "You told us we didn't have to own the land our places sit on to get the buyout."

"You misunderstood the offer," Mitchell said.

"You calling me stupid?"

Destiny stepped between the men. "There will be no name-calling." She pressed a hand against Bernie's chest until he backed up a step and then spoke to the CEO. "Mr. Custer, are you saying the only people eligible to receive the $80,000 payment are those who own land?"

Custer nodded.

Destiny faced her constituents. "That means, only Hank, Melba, Frank and Enrich would receive any money because they own their businesses. The rest of us wouldn't qualify."

A gasp rippled through the saloon. Custer took a swig from the bottle of water Mitchell handed him then said, "I assumed all of you owned the property your trailer sits on."

Bull hockey. The CEO believed he could get this town for next to nothing.

"I'm not moving unless I get paid to move."

"Me, neither."

"Add me to the list of squatters unless I get money."

"Me, too."

"Me, three."

"Me—"

"You told me everyone was on board with my plans!" Custer shouted at Mitchell.

"They were until—" Mitchell nodded to Destiny "—she stirred things up." It took all of Destiny's will-power not to laugh in the men's faces.

"I did what any responsible mayor would do," she said. "I made phone calls, asked questions and uncovered the truth about Wyndell Resorts' offer."

"Don't worry," Melba said. "I'm not selling the motel."

"I've got the best lawyers in the business, and rest assured I'll get my hands on this town," Custer said.

"If you're gonna play dirty, so will I." Melba climbed onto a chair. "Anyone living behind the motel can buy their pad from me for one dollar."

"That raises the buyout to a couple million," Destiny said.

Custer's face turned ruddy. "I'll offer each resident fifty thousand whether they're a landowner or not."

"Take a vote, Destiny," Hank shouted.

"Yeah, let's vote before Mr. CEO changes his mind," Frank said.

"All in favor of selling out, raise your hand." Destiny counted fourteen. "Opposed?" She raised her hand and said, "It's a tie."

"This town needs to think long and hard about its future. Life is short and all of you are nearing the finish line." Custer shoved Mitchell. "If I don't own this town soon, you're fired." Then he spoke to Destiny. "I've never lost a land deal, Ms. Saunders, and I don't intend to start with this town."

When Custer made a move to step past her, she blocked him. "Be prepared for a fight, because I don't give up. Ever."

Custer left the bar, and Destiny grabbed Mitchell's

arm when he tried to follow his boss out the door. "Are there any more questions or comments for Mr. Mitchell?"

"Yeah," Ralph said. "Tell your boss to shove his resort up his you-know-what."

"Anything else?" Destiny said.

Bernie stepped forward. "What happens to Maisy, Victor and Antonio if Custer buys the town?" In addition to being the sheriff, Bernie had been assigned caretaker of the cemetery. "We can't let them desecrate the burial plots," he said.

"I agree. That's bad karma," Melba said. "If I have to leave here, I don't want any ghosts following me."

"I don't know what will happen to the cemetery." Mitchell jerked out of Destiny's hold and left the bar.

"Melba, it was generous of you to offer to sell the trailer pads for a dollar, but you'll need to hire a lawyer to make sure everything is legallike, otherwise Custer's minions will find a loophole." Destiny's eyes landed on Buck, and she wondered what was going through his mind. Her stomach felt queasy so she smiled at the group and said, "Get on with bingo night and have fun." Before her stomach erupted in public, she spun on her heels and left the saloon.

As soon as the door shut behind Destiny, Buck spoke to Hank. "What are the chances of Destiny, or anyone for that matter, stopping Custer?"

"Zero to none," Hank said. "Destiny'll do what she can to slow down the process, but it's only a matter of time before Custer gets his hands on this town. None of us has the resources or legal connections to fight him."

That's what Buck figured. He stood.

"Aren't you playing bingo?" Hank asked.

"Maybe next time." When Buck stepped outside, he spotted Destiny entering the garage. He hurried after her, but got as far as the cemetery before Bernie intercepted him.

"Got me a few questions for you." Bernie turned his head and spit tobacco juice at the ground. "Seems kind of funny…your truck breakin' down and you decidin' to stay in town awhile."

The sheriff should be sharing his concerns with Destiny since she'd stranded Buck.

"Is Custer payin' you to cozy up to Destiny so you can persuade her to sell out?"

Buck felt something bump his ankle and glanced down—a cat was weaving figure eights between his legs.

"Look, Bernie. I don't want to become involved in the town's dispute with Custer. I'm only here until my truck gets fixed, then I'm moving on."

"Maisy would vote against selling out." Bernie stared at the tree in the cemetery.

"Maisy's dead. She doesn't have a say in the town's future." A cold feeling enveloped Buck and he shivered.

"I wouldn't go pissin' off Maisy, if I were you," Bernie said.

Buck didn't believe in ghosts. The cat's purring grew louder and he decided to move on. "See you later." He left Bernie standing in the middle of the street and hurried to the garage. He walked around back and climbed the stairs then knocked on the door.

When the door opened, Buck suddenly lost his voice. Destiny had changed out of her business suit and into a pair of lounging pants that hung low on her hips and a tank top that exposed her tanned belly.

"What is it, Buck?"

The question jarred him out of his stupor. "Got a minute to talk?"

"Sure." She flipped the lock then opened the door. Buck stepped inside the tiny apartment. He noticed two doors off the living area and assumed one was a bedroom and the other a bathroom. The main room was sparsely furnished—only one photograph of a gray-haired couple rested on the sofa table.

"Sit down," she said. "Would you like a drink?"

"I'm good, thanks."

She went into the kitchen area and removed a bottled water from the miniature fridge. There was no stove, only a hot plate and a microwave. She sat in the chair across from the sofa and tucked her feet beneath her. Where was the confident mayor who'd stood up to Custer and Mitchell a short while ago? She looked young and vulnerable, as if she drove a Honda Civic and not the Wide Glide hog parked in the garage.

"Buck?"

He blinked. "What?"

The warmth in her eyes elevated his testosterone another level. "You're staring at me," she said.

"Can't help it. Every time I see you, you look different." He studied her outfit. "I'm trying to figure out what else you are that I don't know yet."

"What do you mean?"

"I've seen the jilted bride, the motorcycle mama, the car mechanic and tonight a mayor."

Her face turned red, and he suspected there was another part to Destiny but she wasn't sharing it. "I ran into Bernie on the way here. He said Maisy doesn't want the town sold."

"Maisy talked to Bernie?"

"I don't believe in ghosts. I'm just conveying his message." Buck cleared his throat. "That was impressive the way you caught Custer off guard when you clarified the payout offer. I think he believed he could pull the wool over everyone's eyes."

"I chitchatted with Custer's secretary before seeing him and she spilled the beans."

"The town needs a lawyer, Destiny."

"We can't afford one."

"There's no way you'll prevent Custer from taking what he wants. If I were you, I'd cast your vote with those who want to sell and negotiate a better deal."

"I'm not giving up on Lizard Gulch."

"You're young and you own a wrecker. You can open a business anywhere."

"Can I?" She jumped up from the chair and paced in front of the couch. "I barely have any savings, certainly not enough to pay the first month's rent for an apartment in Kingman let alone buy a property for my car-repair business."

"Work for someone else until you save enough money."

"I don't want to." She swept her arm in front of her. "This is where I want to live. This is home now."

"I don't understand why a woman your age wants to hang out with old people." He raised his hands. "I have nothing against geriatrics. Shoot, I was raised by my grandparents." He shook his head. "But most women your age are out shopping, barhopping, having fun and looking for Mr. Right to settle down with."

"I have no interest in picking up guys in bars or—"

"What about school? Did you ever consider going to college?"

She shook her head. "Did you?"

"I took a few courses at the junior college but stopped wasting my money when I figured out what I wanted to do."

"You mean rodeo?" she asked.

No. For the past couple of years Buck had talked with his brothers about opening a body shop. He didn't mind working for Troy Winters, but now that he'd seen what Destiny had—her own wrecker and garage… "I mean someday I want to become my own boss." He felt guilty not confessing that he was a mechanic, but not so guilty that he wanted to come clean.

"I make very little money at what I do, but I like that I don't have to answer to anyone but me," she said.

"Maybe you should negotiate a better deal for yourself with Custer," Buck said. "If you convince everyone in town not to fight him, he might compensate you even though you don't own the property the garage sits on."

She scowled. "I would never use the others to gain an advantage for myself."

"I don't get it," he said. "You're not related to any of these people, and they've lived here longer than you have. Why all the concern over what happens to them?"

"They don't have anywhere to go. Most of them are estranged from their families," she said.

He admired Destiny for her generosity and concern, which made him think of his grandparents and how they'd never banned Buck's mother from coming home regardless of how many times she'd gotten pregnant.

"Don't worry about us. I have another month before

Custer puts the heat on." She sounded confident, but Buck read the worry in her eyes.

"What are your plans for tomorrow?" he asked.

"Nothing, why?"

"Let's get out of here."

"Where do you want to go?"

"I've never seen Devil's Lake south of Flagstaff," he said.

She nibbled her lower lip, and Buck worried she was thinking of excuses not to go. He stepped closer—close enough that he could tuck a curl behind her ear. His fingertip lingered against her soft skin a second before he brushed his lips against hers.

Her sigh spurred him on, and he deepened the kiss. When they came up for air, her eyes remained closed.

"Okay," she whispered. "We'll go to the lake tomorrow."

Chapter Six

"I thought we were going to Devil's Lake today." Buck's voice rang out inside the garage Thursday morning.

"We are." Destiny wiped her hands on her coveralls. She'd risen at the crack of dawn to fix the axel she'd taken apart on Buck's truck. She'd been an idiot to strand him in town. Last night when he'd kissed her, she'd realized she'd gotten in over her head with the sexy cowboy. She'd tossed and turned in bed, imagining all the things she'd like to do with him—the sort of things a pregnant woman probably shouldn't think about. She'd woken this morning determined to send Buck on his way—after their picnic.

"I discovered I had the parts I needed in my storage bins, so I canceled the order for the new axel." *An axel she'd never ordered in the first place.*

"Is that so?" Buck sounded as if he didn't believe her.

"Take a look if you want."

Buck lay down on the creeper and slid under the truck then ten seconds later he reappeared. "You weren't kidding."

"After the trip to Devil's Lake you can take off." The sooner he left, the sooner she could focus on finding a way to prevent Lizard Gulch from being bulldozed off the map.

"How much time do you need to get ready?" he asked.

"None." She ripped apart the snaps of the coveralls, revealing a tank top and jean shorts. She nodded to his feet. "Do you have other shoes besides cowboy boots?"

"I've got a pair of running shoes. I keep them in the truck in case I twist my ankle when I rodeo."

She stared at his jeans. "Are you wearing swim trunks under those?"

"I didn't know you wanted to swim."

"We might as well since we're driving all the way up there," she said.

"We'll stop at the motel room on the way out of town, and I'll grab the trunks Melba loaned me for the pool party."

She reached for the keys to the Harley.

"Let's take my truck." He retrieved the cooler he'd left at the end of the repair bay. "I bought sandwiches and drinks. If we're out in the sun all day the air-conditioning will feel good."

Destiny caught the way Buck's gazed roamed over her body, and she wondered if he suspected she was pregnant. *No.* If he thought she might be expecting, he wouldn't have kissed her last night. Regardless, his offer made sense, especially in her condition. "Okay, we'll take the pickup."

Fifteen minutes later they were headed out of town with cool air blasting in Destiny's face. The first twenty minutes of the ride she answered Buck's questions about the town's residents, then the next thing she knew he was shaking her shoulder.

"What?" She blinked. "Are we here?"

"You fell asleep in the middle of our conversation."

How embarrassing. "Sorry."

He parked in a lot not far from the lake then shut off the engine, hopped out and opened her door. Daryl had never been this considerate. When it came to men maybe she should set the bar higher.

"If you don't mind waiting—" Buck pointed to the public restrooms across the parking lot "—I'll change into my trunks and leave my jeans in the pickup."

"Sure, go ahead." Destiny used the few minutes alone to gather her wits and wake up. She hoped falling asleep at the drop of a dime wasn't going to plague her through the entire pregnancy. It was bad enough that she suffered morning sickness during the day.

When Buck returned, he grabbed the cooler and they entered the trail. As they walked side-by-side in comfortable silence, she mulled over the craziness of the past week. Had it only been six days since she'd come upon Buck on the side of the road? It felt as though she'd known him much longer.

"Be careful." He guided her past a rock that jutted into the path.

When they got their first view of the lake, Destiny said, "It's bigger than I imagined."

"I didn't know boats were allowed on the water," he said. A houseboat floated in the middle of the lake. The heavy scent of burning charcoal wafted through the air as families and children crowded the beach area, playing in the sand and cooking on portable grills.

Buck shielded his eyes from the sun. "Where do you want to sit?"

"What about the rocks over there." She indicated the large boulders at the far side of the beach area.

Holding hands they walked through the crowd. He helped Destiny step onto the lower rocks then up to a larger boulder shaded by a tree. They spread their towels across the stone and sat.

"This is perfect," she said. In too many ways that were dangerous.

He opened the cooler and handed her a water. They people-watched for a few minutes, then Buck spoke. "Aren't you going to take off your T-shirt and shorts?" The sparkle in his eyes hinted at mischief.

"Are you eager to get me out of my clothes?" She kept a straight face.

"I want to see the tattoo peeking out of your swimsuit top." He grinned. "I couldn't tell for sure what it was at the pool party."

She whipped off her shirt.

"You're wearing your scary bikini."

She laughed. "Scary?"

"Most people think skulls and crossbones are morbid."

She moved aside the material, revealing a flower. Buck caught her off guard when he traced the petals, his touch setting off a series of quivers in her belly. "I thought this might be an animal tail, but they're bluebells."

"Most guys don't know one flower from the next." She straightened the bikini before Buck's finger found its way farther inside her top.

"My grandmother kept a wildflower garden," he said. "She was always frustrated that she couldn't grow bluebells in the desert."

"Tell me more about your family," she said.

"We're an interesting bunch. My siblings and I all have different fathers."

"After the childhood I had," she said, "not much shocks me."

"My mother believed the perfect man for her was out there somewhere and she spent her whole life searching for him."

"My mother hated men, but she needed them to survive." Needed their money and was willing to do anything for a buck.

"Even when my mom came home for a few months, she never really acted like a mother," he said.

"How did you get along with your father?"

Buck stared into space. "I don't know who my father is."

"You never asked your mother?"

"She said she'd tell me if I wanted to know. I asked her if my father had ever contacted her about wanting to see me, and when she said no, I told her that I didn't have any interest in connecting with him."

"You aren't the least bit curious about the man?"

"Nope. He's known all these years where I live and not once has he made an effort to see me." Buck slapped at an imaginary fly on his arm. "He isn't worth my worry or concern."

"I wish I didn't care about my father," she said.

"Who is he?"

"I have no idea. My mother gave me the first names of two of her regular customers as possible candidates in case I wanted to try and track them down."

"First names?"

"She never asked the last name of the men she had

sex with." Destiny expected to see repulsion not sympathy in Buck's eyes. "We lived in one truck stop for six months until a police officer caught my mother turning tricks in the bathroom. We moved on to another place after that."

"You had a tough go of it. I resented my mother for leaving us kids for months at a time, but I had my grandparents and the farm was home. I can't imagine what your day-to-day life was like."

"It could have been worse. There were people along the way that helped me and my mother. We got free meals at the restaurants in the truck stops and they pretended they didn't know we used the showers. One waitress brought my mother a bag of used children's clothing for me." Destiny smiled. "Inside that bag was a pink dress with ruffles. I felt like a real princess when I wore it."

Buck had the urge to touch her but held back, uncertain if she'd appreciate his sympathy. "I can't picture you in ruffles."

"I was five and believed my mother's lies."

"What lies?"

"That one day we'd have a real home and I'd have a father. That we'd be part of a family. And she promised me I'd ride the school bus like all the other kids."

"But it never happened," Buck said.

"No."

"Did your mother ever reach out for help? What about putting you in foster care if she couldn't take care of you?"

"I was ten the first time I threatened to run away, but she guilted me into staying, insisting I was her only reason for living."

"That's a lot to put on a kid."

"For all my mom's faults, she never did hard drugs or drank herself stupid. And even though she claimed she hated men, I think sex with strangers was her addiction."

"Did the Carters check into your mother's whereabouts after they took you in?"

"Before the Carters were able to adopt me, social services made an attempt to locate my mother but they never found her."

"Do you think something bad happened to her?"

"Maybe. I don't think about her anymore." Destiny nudged his arm. "What about your mother? Do you see much of her?"

"She passed away when I was teenager. Grandma believed it was from a broken heart."

"No man will ever break my heart, that's for sure."

"Daryl didn't even put a dent in it?"

"Nope."

"If you didn't love him, why'd you two set a wedding date?"

She couldn't tell Buck that they'd agreed to marry because of the baby. "People get married for all sorts of reasons." How had the conversation switched from mothers to Destiny's botched marriage plans? "Back to my mother...I'm not saying the way she raised me was right, but after I'd settled in with the Carters, I noticed plenty of other kids had it worse than me. I hadn't been beaten or abused, and none of the men my mother had sex with ever raped me. For that I'll always be grateful."

"Your mother stole your childhood from you."

"I've put those years behind me and moved on. Besides, Lizard Gulch is the home I've always dreamed of."

"But for how long?"

"I'm not giving up the fight to save the town," she said.

"Men with money and influence like Custer and Mitchell play dirty and never get caught."

"I won't let them steal our home out from under us," she said, even though Buck had made a valid point. Custer would do everything in his power—legal or not—to get his hands on Lizard Gulch.

"If Custer wins, where will you go?" Buck asked.

"I don't know."

"Your best bet would be to move to Phoenix or Tucson and look for towing jobs."

"I don't just want to tow cars. I enjoy being a mechanic, too." Her heart sped up when Buck's gaze drifted to her mouth. For an instant she forgot they were visiting a lake along with hundreds of other people.

"Destiny," he said.

"What?"

"You're not like any girl I've known."

"And I bet you've known a lot of girls." Buck's handsome face and engaging personality undoubtedly attracted women of all ages. Curious, she asked, "What kind of girls do you prefer?"

"I've mostly dated country girls."

She envisioned a blonde with pigtails running through a pecan grove. "I bet you like the Goody Two-shoes girls."

"I've dated plenty of those gals." He tugged one of her curls. "Everything about you warns me away, but I can't stop—" he leaned closer "—thinking about kissing you."

Her heart pounded as the scent of his aftershave filled her head. She smoothed her fingers across his cheek fascinated by the gold flecks sparkling in his brown eyes. In that instant she wished she was someone else—anyone but a pregnant unwed mother-to-be, about to lose her home and livelihood.

She sighed when his lips caressed hers. It would be so easy to fall in love with Buck. Sylvia had invited Destiny to live with her in Florida after Simon died but she'd been ready to strike out on her own. When she'd landed in Lizard Gulch, she'd found a family of misfits willing to take her in, and she was grateful for their kindness toward her. As much as she considered them family, she yearned for the love of a good man—a man she and her child could build a life with.

You won't find that man if you hide out in Lizard Gulch.

Buck angled his head and deepened the kiss, teasing her with the tip of his tongue. She snuggled closer, losing herself in his embrace. Today she'd enjoy being with Buck, pretending they were a couple with their own happy-ever-after waiting for them on the other side of the lake.

BY THE TIME Buck parked his truck behind the garage, darkness had fallen. After he and Destiny spent the afternoon at the lake, they'd stopped at the Rocky Mountain Café thirty miles east of Lizard Gulch and eaten supper. For such a small thing, she'd packed the food away and then when they'd hit the road again, she'd fallen asleep.

Destiny was a tough girl with plenty of street smarts and comfortable in her own skin. She was the kind of woman a man could spend the night with and not have to worry about an uncomfortable morning-after scene. He wanted to take her upstairs right now, but he'd caught the look of vulnerability in her eyes when she'd talked about her mother and childhood and he'd thought maybe she needed a friend more than a lover right now.

He opened his door and the interior cab light went on. "Destiny."

Her lashes fluttered up.

"We're home." He'd meant to say *you're* home. He ignored the Freudian slip and blamed it on missing the farm and his siblings.

"I dozed off." She pressed the back of her hand against her mouth and yawned.

"Did you know that you snore?" he said. "Like a tow-truck driver."

"I do not." Her gaze shifted to the street. "Are you leaving tonight?"

Buck had no reason to stay, except that he wasn't ready to say goodbye to Destiny. "Tomorrow's soon enough. It's late and I have to settle my bill with Melba, not to mention paying you for fixing my truck."

A pink tinge spread across her cheeks. "It's on the house."

No doubt she felt guilty about tampering with the axel on his pickup. "How do you expect to make a living if you don't charge your customers?"

Rather than answer him she got out of the truck.

"I'll walk you up to the apartment."

"Thanks, but I don't need an escort."

Always the tough girl.

"In case you leave before I wake tomorrow…it was nice knowing you, Buck. Good luck with your rodeo-ing." She walked away before he found the words to stop her.

He doubted he'd get much sleep tonight so he headed to Lucille's for a beer. He stopped when he reached the cemetery and peered through the darkness at the head-stones. He didn't understand how Bernie made a liv-ing off ghost tours. The sheriff would be lucky if he gave one tour a year. Switching directions, he skirted the gate enclosing the plots and the famous hangman's tree then knocked on Bernie's trailer.

"Be right there." The door opened a crack—enough to let out a handful of cats.

Loud meowing echoed through the darkness, and Buck raised his voice to be heard over the racket. "I'm leaving town in the morning and I wondered if I could take a ghost tour."

"Tonight?"

"Isn't that the usual time to take a ghost tour—when it's dark outside?"

"Hold your horses." The door closed in Buck's face.

He walked to the front of the cemetery and waited. The same cold feeling he'd gotten before when he'd stood by the cemetery racked his body. He had a feeling he was no longer alone, but there wasn't a soul in sight.

"That's Maisy," Bernie said, approaching from the opposite direction, several cats marching behind him.

"What do you mean, it's Maisy?" Buck asked.

"She likes to stand next to people on the tour."

Buck studied Bernie's outfit. He'd pinned his star to the lapel of his 1960s tuxedo jacket, which he wore over his baggy jeans. He'd donned a top hat and held a key in his hand.

"What's the key for?"

"To unlock the gate."

Buck stared at the iron fence surrounding the graves. "I don't see a lock."

"Go ahead and try the gate," Bernie said.

Buck pushed against the opening, but it didn't budge. He pulled—no luck. "How the hell can that be?"

Bernie crooked a fuzzy eyebrow as if Buck was dense in the head.

"Where do you insert the key?" Buck asked.

"I don't. We stand here until Maisy decides to let us in."

"Then why the heck do you need a key?"

"People like the drama."

Buck swallowed a groan. "How long do we wait for—" A squeaky sound interrupted him. "Did you hear that?"

"That's Maisy's signal to go in." Bernie pushed against the gate and it swung open.

Buck followed his guide to the first grave—Victor Candor's. He read the birth and death date. "Victor was fifty-six."

"Maisy was twenty-four at the time of her death," Bernie said.

Buck stared at Antonio Torres's marker. "He was just a kid. Twenty-one years old."

"Most folks believe Maisy planned to marry Victor for his money, but—" Bernie stumbled forward and Buck steadied him.

"Damn broad," Bernie grumbled. "She gets pushy when I tell the truth." He straightened his jacket. "Antonio came through town on his way to Los Angeles. He was from the Bronx, New York, and Maisy fell hard for the Puerto Rican's good looks and accent. Antonio talked Maisy into running away with him, but Victor found out and confronted Antonio."

Buck wasn't sure if he believed the story of Maisy and her lovers, but after listening to Destiny's account of the threesome and now Bernie's, it was obvious everyone in town told the same story. "Sounds like a Hollywood movie script."

Bernie went over to the tree and batted a hand at a rope, hanging off one of the larger branches. "This ain't the same rope Maisy hung herself with. Someone stole the real one years ago." The cats circled the tree, meowing. "Maisy's cat, Henry, slept next to this tree for weeks after she died," Bernie said. "Then one night he up and disappeared."

"Destiny said there's a rumor that sometimes people can hear Maisy calling for her lovers at night."

Bernie cocked his head as if trying to hear voices from beyond the grave. Then he blinked. "You got any questions?"

"That's the whole ghost tour?" Buck asked.

"These here are the only ghosts we got in Lizard Gulch."

What a rip-off. "How much do I owe you?"

"Ten dollars."

Buck opened his wallet and removed two five-dollar bills.

Bernie shut the gate behind them.

"What about the cats?" The felines had sprawled out beneath tree, tails swishing.

"They'll come out when Henry leaves."

"Those female cats?"

"Yep."

"Henry must be a Don Juan," Buck said.

"See you tomorrow." Bernie retreated inside his trailer and shut off the porch light.

No longer in the mood for a beer, Buck walked over to the motel, ignoring the uncomfortable pressure he felt pushing against his back. *You're imagining things.* Just in case he wasn't… "Don't mess with me, Maisy."

He entered his room and turned on the lights—they flickered twice, then everything went dark. He flipped the switch again—more flickering, then darkness. *Maisy?*

The lights popped on but there were no remnants of mists or shadows in the room. "This is crazy. I don't believe in ghosts." He went into the bathroom and squeezed a dollop of toothpaste onto his brush, but as soon as he looked at his image in the mirror, the lights went off again.

He finished cleaning his teeth in the dark then when he returned to the main room, the lights came on. The motel was old—maybe when Melba turned the other rooms into her private living quarters, the construction crew messed up the electrical system. He stood at the window and stared down the street toward Destiny's garage. A shadow moved past the apartment window above the work bay.

I don't want to leave.

There's nothing for you to do here.

Since he'd hit the road at the beginning of the summer, Buck had enjoyed the respite from working on cars with Troy. Then he'd run into Destiny and had seen her garage, and now he was itching to get his hands dirty again. But did he want to go back and work for Troy?

Maybe…maybe not. The one thing he knew for sure was that he'd been away from home long enough. He needed to patch things up with Will and see his new niece, Addy.

The lights flickered wildly then an instant later he swore he heard a gunshot. His hand automatically went to his chest, patting himself in search of a wound that wasn't there. He must be imagining things. He shucked out of his clothes and slid beneath the bedcovers.

Right as he drifted off to sleep the muffled sound of a door slamming met his ears. Tomorrow he'd check with Melba about the lights and ask if one of her tenants in the trailer park got his kicks firing off a gun late at night.

Chapter Seven

Destiny stared at the crumpled front end of Bernie's 1967 black Plymouth GTX that she'd towed into the garage after he'd knocked on her door at the crack of dawn asking for help. He'd crashed the car during a joyride and had walked two miles back to town. "How did this happen again?"

"I told you. I felt like taking a drive—"

"At four-thirty in the morning?"

"I had to get out of my place. Those damned cats wouldn't stop meowing after I gave a ghost tour last night."

"Who took the tour?"

"Buck."

Poor Buck. He must have been bored out of his mind.

"It was the darnedest thing," Bernie said. "The steering wheel just locked up and I couldn't turn the car. At least the brakes worked, and I wasn't going that fast when I hit the boulder."

"I can do the engine repairs but not the body work." The fender, headlights and hood had sustained considerable damage. "You'll need to contact your insurance company to—"

"I don't have insurance, and I can't afford to take it

into one of those fancy collision centers in Kingman. Can you pound out the worst of the dents?"

A low whistle rent the air and Destiny and Bernie glanced up from studying the car. Buck strolled into the garage, looking well rested and sexy as all get out. Destiny braced herself—he'd come to say a final goodbye, and she refused to act all stupid when she sent him off with a smile and a nice-knowing-you hug.

"What the heck happened, Bernie?" he asked.

"What does it look like? I crashed my car."

"That's a shame." Buck circled the vehicle, eyeing the damage. "The GTX was a beauty."

Destiny noticed Buck's pickup wasn't parked outside. He must have walked from the motel. "I guess you're ready to hit the road."

"Mind if I have a word in private with Destiny?" Buck spoke to Bernie.

The sheriff retreated to the office and switched on the TV. Left alone with Buck, Destiny resisted fidgeting when he peered intently at her face. She hadn't slept a wink last night, wondering if their paths would ever cross again.

"I can help you with Bernie's car," he said.

Her mouth went dry. Maybe Buck didn't want to leave town—or her. "You don't know a thing about cars—you said so yourself."

He stared at the toe of his cowboy boot. "I wasn't exactly truthful with you when you asked me that question last week."

He locked gazes with her and she felt light-headed. "You lied to me?"

"I'm a certified mechanic," he said. "When I'm not

rodeoing, I work for a friend who owns a car repair business."

Embarrassed, she resisted touching her burning face for fear the skin would melt onto her hands. "What kind of mechanic?"

"Mostly engines but I've done body work on occasion."

Oh, God. "So you know…"

"That you stranded me in Lizard Gulch on purpose?" He inched closer, his fresh-from-the-shower scent overwhelming her. "No woman's ever tried to hold me hostage." His brown-eyed stare bored into her. "I'm glad you did."

She ignored the blip in her heartbeat, more certain now than ever that he had to leave. But when she opened her mouth to tell him to go, the words caught in her throat.

"Let me help you work on Bernie's car," he said.

"I don't have the money to pay you."

"I'll take room and board in exchange for my labor."

"What's wrong with your motel room?" Besides costing him money.

"I don't like my roommate."

Destiny chuckled. "Is Maisy bothering you?"

"Hey, I don't believe in ghosts, but last night I swore I heard a gun go off."

"You didn't hear this from me…" Destiny lowered her voice. "Melba and Bernie are behind all the ghost pranks."

"What? Why would they do that?"

"Beats me. I think Melba gets a kick out of scaring people and Bernie plays along because he can make a few bucks off ignorant tourists who happen to stumble upon the town."

"So everyone in Lizard Gulch knows the story of Maisy and her lovers is a ruse?"

"The story is true. As for the lights flickering and the gun firing off," Destiny said, "all for show."

Bernie poked his head out of the office. "You gonna fix my car or not?"

Destiny ignored him and spoke to Buck. "If you stay and help me you won't be able to rodeo."

"There'll be other rodeos."

"Your family?" If she had a family like Buck's, she wouldn't want to be away from them for any length of time.

"Don't worry, they don't miss me."

He doesn't want to leave. Destiny yearned to accept his offer, but if he moved in with her, there was no telling what would happen between them. He wasn't a man a woman could ignore—not even a pregnant one. "How long will it take you to pound out the dents in Bernie's car?"

"Two or three weeks if you have the right tools. Longer if you don't."

C'mon. You know you want him to stay.

"It might be a good idea to keep me here," he said.

"Why's that?"

"With Custer causing trouble for the town, my help would give you more free time to take care of your mayoral responsibilities."

Hire him, Destiny. What could it hurt? "You'd have to sleep on my couch."

"That's better than paying fifty dollars a night at the motel."

"Okay. You can bunk down in my apartment in exchange for working on Bernie's car."

"You won't regret this." His smile promised her that she would.

Destiny entered her office to give Bernie the news. "Buck says he can fix the dents in your car, but it'll take at least—" An unfamiliar vehicle pulled up in front of the motel and she walked over to the front window to get a better look. "Who's that?"

Bernie pressed his face against the glass. "Never seen 'em before."

Mitchell emerged from the car. "What's he doing here?" she said.

"Looks like he brought reinforcements with him," Bernie said when a couple came into view. "Think I'll mosey on down there and find out."

Mitchell escorted the man and woman into the motel office. She'd find out soon enough who they were. Spinning on her heels she went back into the garage and found Buck beneath the Plymouth.

"The fuel pump's damaged," he said.

Destiny rubbed her brow, already regretting her decision to hire Buck. The last thing she needed was another man telling her how to do her job.

"THE MUSIC SURE is loud over at Lucille's," Destiny said.

Buck had been watching her the past hour while they took apart the engine in the Plymouth. She was antsy, and he worried that she regretted hiring him and inviting him to crash on her couch.

A rumbling sound echoed near his ear. "Sorry." She pressed a hand against her tummy.

"You're hungry." He checked his watch. "It's four-thirty. You want to call it a day?"

"Sure."

They pushed their creepers out into the open and stood. "What do you say I treat you to dinner at Lucille's after we clean up?" he said.

"Thanks, but there's a frozen pizza in the freezer with my name on it."

"Skip the pizza and meet me at Lucille's in a half hour." He walked out before Destiny had a chance to protest. Back in his motel room he showered and changed into a clean pair of jeans and a T-shirt. He had a couple more outfits left in his duffel, before he had to find a place to do laundry.

When he stepped outside his room, Melba was waiting for him. "Did you hear?"

"Hear what?"

"We've got visitors in town."

"Tourists, movie stars or freelance reporters?" he asked.

"Jim and Delores Docker. They're from Pennsylvania."

"It's a little early for snowbirds, isn't it?"

"They're friends of Mitchell."

That couldn't be good.

"I don't know their story," Melba said. "They're eating supper at Lucille's tonight."

"I'm meeting Destiny there. I'll walk over with you." After they crossed the parking lot, he said, "I'm checking out of my room tonight."

"You're leaving? Bernie said you were fixing his car."

"I'm staying awhile longer, but Destiny offered me

her couch in exchange for working on the Plymouth." He sent Melba an innocent look. "Last night I swore I heard gunfire."

"Really? I didn't hear a thing."

"And the lights kept flickering on and off." Buck struggled not to laugh. "It happened right after I took a ghost tour with Bernie." He stopped in the middle of the street. "You don't think Maisy followed me back to my room?"

Melba's eyes twinkled. "Destiny told you, didn't she?"

"So it was you playing with the lights?"

Melba continued walking. "I have a master switch in my apartment."

"What about the gun firing?" he asked.

"I shoot a blank into a pillow."

"So everyone knows when they hear a gunshot that you're the estranged shooter?"

"Nope. Just Bernie and Destiny. The others believe the ghosts of Victor and Antonio are shooting at each other." She tugged on his shirtsleeve. "You can't tell anyone."

"Your secret's safe with me." When they reached the steps to the saloon he asked, "What about the Dockers? You don't plan to scare them, do you?"

"Hell yes, I do." Melba winked then entered the bar.

Lucille's was hopping—everyone in town must have heard about the Dockers and stopped in to get a look at the couple.

"Melba!" Mitchell waved.

Buck followed the motel manager across the room. Melba stopped in front of the middle-aged couple and introduced him. "This here is Buck Owens Cash."

Mitchell hooted and shook his head. "Every time I hear your name I laugh."

Buck curled his hands into fists then relaxed his fingers. His reaction had been instinctive—ingrained in him from years of ridicule by classmates and rodeo competitors.

"Buck Owens was one of my grandmother's favorites," Docker's wife said. "She saw him in person on *The Ed Sullivan Show*."

Mitchell gestured toward the lady. "This is Delores Docker and her husband, Jim."

Buck shook hands with the couple.

"Mark said you're from Pennsylvania. What part?" Melba asked.

"We live in the Society Hill Historic District in Philadelphia." Delores squeezed her husband's arm. "Jim has his own law practice there."

Another lawyer.

"Hasn't Destiny fixed your truck yet?" Mitchell asked.

"She has, but I'll be sticking around a little longer."

Mitchell frowned. "You're not thinking of moving here, are you?"

Before Buck decided how to answer the question, Destiny appeared at his side, wearing cutoff shorts and a tank top that showed her lizard tattoo. She'd secured her curls to the top of her head with a clip but several strands had fallen free. She looked sexy, and Buck decided he'd rather order his food to go and eat in Destiny's apartment than sit in the bar.

"Who are you?" Destiny spoke to the Dockers.

"This is Jim and Delores Docker from some historic district in Philadelphia. They're passing through town," Melba said.

"Mitchell has told us great things about Lizard Gulch," Jim said. "My wife and I have been searching for a place to buy a winter home."

"You mean trailer," Melba said.

"Pardon?" Delores said.

"We don't have any houses in Lizard Gulch, just mobile homes and two apartments," Melba said. "One above the gas station, which belongs to Destiny, and the other one is over the pastry shop next door."

Jim and Mitchell exchanged a smirk. "The Dockers are staying at the motel while they decide where to build," Mitchell said.

"How long you two planning to be here?" Melba directed the question to Delores.

"A day or two."

"You ought to stay longer than that," Melba said, "especially if you're thinking about moving here for the winters."

"I wouldn't, if I were you," Destiny said.

"Why not?" Delores asked.

Destiny glared at Mitchell. "Didn't you tell them we're being pushed out by a land developer?"

Delores slapped a hand against her bosom, and Buck almost laughed out loud at her feigned shock.

"You're jumping to conclusions, Destiny." Mitchell took Delores by the arm. "Let me introduce you both to the others."

After the group walked off, Destiny said, "There's something stinky about the Dockers showing up out of the blue."

"I know what he's trying to do," Buck said.

"Me, too," Melba chimed in.

"Me, three," Destiny said.

"Mitchell brought them here to break the tie." Buck nodded to the Dockers. "I wonder how much he's paying for their vote."

"What are we gonna do?" Melba asked.

"Destiny can't do a thing about it now," Buck said. "Let's eat." The three of them sat at the bar and ordered burgers and onion rings. Since Melba was eating with them, Buck didn't suggest they take their food to go.

"Damn, Mitchell plays dirty," Destiny said.

"We could drive into Kingman and recruit more residents," Melba said.

"We have to discourage the Dockers from wanting to move here." Destiny chewed an onion ring and swallowed. "If we can't then we'll have to consider Melba's suggestion."

"Force them out," Buck said.

"I'm tempted to sic our sheriff on them." Destiny finished her burger in record time.

"For such a small thing you sure can pack away the food." Buck slapped a twenty-dollar bill on the bar.

"May I have everyone's attention?" Mitchell stood at the front of the room. "Now that you've all met Lizard Gulch's newest residents—" he indicated the Dockers "—I'd like to—"

"Excuse me, Mark." Destiny slid off her stool. "The Dockers aren't residents yet. They have to move here first."

"Building permits take time. Let's not get bogged down in the details, *Destiny*."

"Where are they building a house?" Enrick asked.

Mitchell's smile grew strained. "They haven't decided on a location yet."

"They can't build next to me and Ralph, because I use that lot for a garden," Sonja said.

"They're not moving in behind the motel," Mitchell said.

"Why's that?" Someone in the back of the room spoke. "Are they too good to live next to the rest of us?"

The Dockers were no longer smiling.

"I'm glad you've all had a chance to meet Jim and Delores." Mitchell hopped off the chair. "I'm sure they'd like to get settled in their room now."

Melba looked at Buck. "Buck hasn't moved his things out yet."

"It'll only take me a minute," Buck said.

"The room will need to be cleaned," Melba said.

"That's fine," Delores said, heading for the door. "We can wait."

The Dockers left, Mitchell right on their heels.

"They'll stay long enough to cast a vote at the next town meeting then mysteriously disappear," Destiny said.

"Maybe we should roll out the red carpet," Melba said. "We'll show them how neighborly we all are."

"Kill them with kindness?" Destiny smiled.

Buck swallowed a groan when the two females bent their heads and whispered ideas back and forth.

"What about Custer? What if he shows up out of the blue again and demands a vote?" Buck asked.

"He can demand all the votes he wants—" Destiny planted her hands on her hips "—but no vote is legal until the official monthly meeting."

"When is that meeting?" Buck asked.

"The second week in September."

Buck checked the calendar on his cell phone. "Three weeks from now."

"Maybe by then the Dockers will decide they're better off toughing out the winters in Pennsylvania," Destiny said.

"I better get over to the motel." Melba walked off

"You ready to get out of here?" Destiny asked.

"After you."

Outside the bar Buck said, "Wait here while I get my stuff."

"Sure."

It took him two minutes to gather his belongings and meet up with Destiny in the street. "I'll move my truck down to the garage tomorrow."

They walked side by side, her arm bumping into his every few steps. "Clear sky tonight," he said.

She didn't speak, and he wondered if she was nervous about sharing her apartment with him. They climbed the fire escape then she paused at the door.

"What's the matter?" Was she worried he'd want certain privileges because she'd agreed to allow him to sleep on her couch?

"Buck."

"What?"

"We should discuss the rules before we go in."

He inched closer. "What rules?"

"I'm not sure what you expect from me, but—"

"Hey." He caressed her cheek. "I don't expect anything but a pillow and a bath towel." Buck's words sounded sincere, but his eyes claimed he wanted more.

A huge part of Destiny yearned to give in to her attraction to him, but she was afraid if she did, she'd never be the same again. She didn't want to spend the rest of her life wishing she was the kind of girl a man like Buck might want a happy ever after with.

"Fine," she said. "But keep your clothes on."

"Do the guys you invite over walk around naked in front of you?" His eyes gleamed with humor.

"No."

"Not even Daryl?"

Daryl? She'd all but forgotten the father of her child.

"Anything else?" Buck asked.

"Put the toilet seat down after you use it."

"Yes, ma'am." He grinned.

"Wash your own dishes."

"Agreed."

"I get to use the bathroom first in the morning." Destiny had to, because she threw up as soon as she opened her eyes. Good grief, how would she hide her retching from Buck?

"Don't eat me out of house and home."

"I'll eat most of my meals at Lucille's. Anything else?"

She wanted to tell him that there was no lock on the bedroom door and he'd better not enter her room at night, but her lips wouldn't move.

"What about kissing," he asked.

The air seeped from her lungs. "What about…it?"

"Is kissing off-limits?"

"I don't know." Did that breathy voice really belong to her?

He leaned in, the scent of cologne and pure male making her dizzy. "Why don't I kiss you, then you decide if it's allowed or not."

He nuzzled her lips in a gentle caress. When she thought he might pull away, he deepened the embrace, using his tongue. When he ended the kiss, he whispered, "Take your time thinking it over."

She didn't have to mull anything over—she wanted his kisses. She poked her finger in his chest and put on a brave face. "I'm nothing like those girl-next-door types you've dated in the past. You better watch yourself, because I'm more than you can handle."

The gauntlet had been thrown.

Now which one of them would cave first?

Chapter Eight

Destiny stood next to the supply cabinet in the garage and pretended to search for a socket wrench while she watched Buck out of the corner of her eye. Three days had passed since he'd moved into her apartment and nothing had happened.

Nada.

Zero.

Zilch.

The past three days had been the most disappointing of her life. Maybe she'd scared Buck off when she'd warned him she was more than he could handle. If she expected him to make the first pass, she'd better drop a few hints that she wouldn't bite his head off if he came near her.

The man had been nothing if not the perfect houseguest. He'd done everything she'd asked of him—allowed her to use the bathroom first in the morning. Washed his dishes and didn't leave his clothes lying on the floor. He'd even taken the trash out to the burn barrel. If not for the fact that he slept in his BVDs and walked through the apartment with his shirt hanging open so she caught glimpses of his six-pack abs, she'd swear he was immune to her. And the funny thing—

not funny but pathetic—was that he was aware of her every move, yet he kept his distance.

He's too much of a gentleman.

Destiny hadn't had a lot of experience with *gentlemen*. As a matter of fact, Buck was the first guy she'd been around who had manners and morals. Because of the environment in which her mother had raised her, Destiny expected men to take what they wanted and think only about themselves. To say the least, she had thick skin when it came to the opposite sex and that probably accounted for her not being upset that Daryl had changed his mind about marrying her.

Buck was a man who happened along once in a girl's lifetime and if she wanted to make memories with him, then she'd better do something soon before he discovered her secret. She had a sneaking suspicion that if he knew she was expecting, he'd jump in his pickup and leave Lizard Gulch in the dust.

Buck's cell phone beeped again. It had beeped on and off all morning, and she wondered if he was sexting with a former girlfriend. Since he was lying on the creeper beneath the Plymouth, his face remained hidden from view, and she couldn't tell if he was amused or irritated by all the messages.

"You feel like going for a drive?" Buck rolled into the open and hopped off the board.

"Why?"

He held up his phone. "My sister's been bugging me all morning."

Destiny ignored the twinge of relief she experienced at learning Buck had been texting back and forth with his sister and not a sexy siren.

"Dixie and her husband are heading up to Bullhead

City to visit friends for the weekend, and she wants to meet with me for a few minutes."

"Meet where?" she asked.

"Along I-40 outside of Kingman."

Panic dug its claws into Destiny. Buck wanted her to meet his sister—what did that mean? Shoot, she'd yet to meet Daryl's mother in Denver and Destiny was having his baby. "Umm…"

"You'll appreciate Dixie," he said. "She's a lot like you—she's honest and up-front with people."

Destiny didn't want to like Dixie, let alone meet his family. "I have things to do." She gestured to the tools littering the garage floor.

"You and I both know we can't do much more on the car until the parts you ordered arrive."

Okay, so she was making up excuses.

Hey, you're the one wanting to move things along with Buck. If you don't go, he might be upset and you'll never get more from him than a peep show before he skips town.

"If you're sure…"

"I'm sure." His smile tweaked her heart.

"Your truck or the Harley?" she asked.

"Let's take your bike."

He wanted to show off for his sister. "When do you want to leave?"

"As soon as possible. She'll probably beat us there."

Destiny unsnapped her coveralls and shrugged out of them. "I'll be right back." She made it as far as the doorway before his voice stopped her.

"Where are you going?"

"To change clothes."

"What's wrong with what you have on?" His warm

gaze ran over her body, and she wished they were going for a ride up in her bedroom. "Dixie's a country girl. She'll be wearing jeans and a T-shirt, too."

Destiny turned. "Do you want to drive?"

"Sure." They walked behind the garage and Destiny handed over the keys then she hopped on the bike. Buck pushed against her until his backside fit snuggly in the cradle of her thighs.

Ignoring the sweet ache between her legs she pressed her breasts against his spine and toyed with his belt loops. *Oh, yeah*—this was going to be an arousing ride. Buck revved the motor then took off down the street. Destiny waved at Frank, who'd stepped out of the pastry shop to smoke a cigarette and chat with Melba and Violet drinking coffee in the rocking chairs.

When they passed the motel, she noticed Lizard Gulch's newest residents walking to their room—Delores making wild hand gestures and Jim scowling. She wondered what had upset them.

Destiny was grateful Buck kept the bike's speed at thirty miles per hour as they traveled along the dirt road. Today had been the first morning in weeks she hadn't vomited. When he turned west onto the highway, he revved the motor and the bike took off. Hot wind blowing in her face, she closed her eyes and rested her cheek against his shoulder. She inhaled bike exhaust, dust and Buck's cologne—heaven.

Each time he shifted gears, the muscles in his back bunched, and the movement teased her breasts, hardening her nipples. Feeling bold, she placed her hands on his hips then slowly—an inch at a time—slid her fingers along the inside of his thighs, stopping only when she felt a groan rumble through his chest.

After they'd been on the road fifteen minutes, Buck stiffened. Destiny peeked over his shoulder and spotted a truck parked on the shoulder up ahead. As they drew closer, she noticed the person standing next to the truck was male not female.

Buck cut across the highway then stopped several yards from the other vehicle. After he shut off the engine, he said. "Looks like my sister played a joke on me."

"What do you mean?"

"That's my brother Will."

Will wasn't smiling. And neither was Buck.

"C'mon. I'll introduce you." He hopped off then steadied her as she swung her leg over the back end of the bike.

She walked alongside Buck, glad her mirrored sunglasses hid her eyes so she could study the brother who made no attempt to hide his surprise at seeing her. Will was shorter than Buck by a couple of inches but had the same broad shoulders and muscular arms. She could tell by his stiff-shoulder posture that he was a serious man.

"Guess Dixie's up to her old tricks." Buck halted in front of Will.

"Don't be mad. I twisted her arm." Will nodded to Destiny. "Are you going to introduce us?"

"Destiny, this is Will. Will, this is Destiny."

She offered her hand. "Nice to meet you."

"What do you want?" Buck kept his voice as neutral as possible, aware of Destiny hanging on his every word.

Will shuffled his feet. "Would you mind if I had a word alone with Buck, Destiny?"

"No problem." She returned to the bike and waited for the brothers to finish their conversation.

"She's not your type," Will said. "How'd you two meet?"

His brother's remark irked Buck. "Marsha isn't your type, but I hear you two are married now."

Will rubbed the back of his neck and stared at the ground. "I admit things between us got heated earlier this summer, but you didn't need to run off."

Buck scoffed.

"We're brothers. We have fights all the time. You shouldn't have left."

"You didn't give me a choice, Will."

"I panicked when I got the letter from Marsha and learned I had a fourteen-year-old son."

Panic was putting it mildly. Will had flipped out.

"I said some things I shouldn't have. It was easier to blame you than to accept that I played a role in my own fate."

Buck wouldn't allow Will to take all the blame. "I was pissed that you thought the worst of me, but I was more upset with myself." When Will didn't interrupt, Buck explained, "I should have told you about Ryan when I'd guessed the truth, but I thought for sure Marsha would keep her promise and come clean with you sooner rather than later."

"I won't lie and say it didn't hurt me that you chose to honor Marsha's wishes and keep me in the dark."

"You always said you didn't want kids and—"

"But I had a right to know I'd fathered a child."

There was nothing Buck could say that would make what he'd done okay. "So where do we go from here?"

"We go back to being brothers. Come home, Buck."

"I will…eventually." His gaze shifted to Destiny. "Right now I'm exactly where I want to be."

"Are you and Destiny…?"

"Not yet, but we're heading in that direction." He hoped. "She's making me rethink what I want in a woman."

Will chuckled. "She looks like a handful."

"I'm up for the challenge."

"Bring her to the farm and introduce her to the family."

"Maybe later. I'm staying here for now."

"Where exactly is *here*?" Will asked.

"Lizard Gulch."

"Never heard of the place."

"Me, neither, until my truck broke down."

"Is that her Harley?"

"Yep."

"Nice machine. Would she let me drive it?"

"Probably, but don't ask her."

Will laughed then sobered. "The family misses you. Johnny wants you to see his new daughter. And Dixie doesn't like it when any of us stray too far."

"I won't be gone much longer." Only time would tell how things would end between him and Ms. Harley.

"Are we good, Buck?" Will asked.

"We're good if you can forgive me for being an ass."

"This isn't the first time and it won't be the last time you're an ass." Will punched Buck in the shoulder then there was an awkward pause before they hugged. "Don't stay away too long." Will waved to Destiny then left in his truck.

"Everything okay between you two?" Destiny asked when Buck reached her side.

He clasped her face between his hands and kissed her. "What was that for?"

"Just making sure," he said then hopped on the bike.

"Making sure of what?" She snuggled closer.

"That you're the reason I'm not going home."

DESTINY FLOATED ON cloud nine as Buck drove them back to Lizard Gulch, her thoughts racing with ways to seduce him. She fantasized about walking out of her bedroom in the wee morning hours, wearing nothing but her bikini panties and a see-through tank top. Or maybe she'd stroll past the couch in her cutoff shorts and sit outside, using the heat in her bedroom as an excuse for needing fresh air.

Her musings were interrupted when Buck drove the Harley into town and she saw a commotion outside Lucille's. "Stop at the bar," she shouted.

After Buck parked, she hopped off the bike in front of the gathering crowd. "What's going on?"

Bernie spoke up. "I was called to settle a disturbance."

"What kind of disturbance?" she asked.

"It's the Dockers." Melba stepped forward. "They're cheating at bingo."

Destiny had forgotten about the weekly event. "It's not six o'clock yet."

"The ladies started early tonight because Mitchell wanted them to include Docker's wife," Bernie said.

"How do you know the Dockers cheated?" Destiny asked.

"We don't exactly have proof," Melba said.

Oh, boy. "How much money have they won so far?"

"Two hundred twenty-five dollars." Melba lifted her

chin. "That may not be a lot to them, but they don't live off of their social security checks like we do."

Destiny hated to see Mitchell's friends take advantage of a group of retirees.

"Want me to arrest them?" Bernie asked.

"That won't be necessary." Destiny wished with all her heart she could ignore the bingo fiasco and flee to her apartment with Buck, lock the door then tumble him on the bed. "Be right back."

"I'm not missing this." Buck followed her inside the bar.

Enrick stood by the bingo machine, calling out the numbers while the Dockers sat alone at a table. Mitchell stood at the bar, drinking a beer.

"Is everyone having a good time?" Destiny shouted above the chatter.

"Haven't had this much fun since I took my law exam back in eighty." Jim's sarcastic joke hit a nerve with Destiny, and no one else in the room laughed.

"I'm glad you're enjoying yourselves." An idea came to mind, and she clapped her hands to get everyone's attention. "Did you inform the Dockers about the new bingo rule the town council passed?"

Blank faces stared at her.

"Remember we decided—" she glanced at the Dockers "—that all winners will donate their money to our fund for…"

"A drive-in movie theater," Melba shouted from the doorway.

"A drive-in?" Jim frowned.

"We're looking for ways to bring tourists to Lizard Gulch. We've got the mini golf course, ghost tours and the pastry shop and saloon, but we needed something to put in that big empty space behind Destiny's garage," Melba said.

"It's too hot to watch movies outside." Delores appeared genuinely befuddled.

"Wait one minute," Mitchell said. "This is the first I've heard of plans for a drive-in." He pointed at Destiny. "You're making this up."

"Am I lying?" Destiny posed the question to the group.

A chorus of "no" echoed through the bar.

"You can't take money from people who win it fair and square," Mitchell argued.

"I'm afraid we can." Bernie puffed up his chest. "And I'm here to enforce the law."

Steam spewed from Mitchell's ears. "I'd like to see the minutes from the meeting where you decided the town needed a drive-in movie theater."

"Melba will get the notes to you when she has time," Destiny said.

"Never mind," Mitchell grumbled. "She'll just forge the minutes."

Destiny wanted to laugh at Mitchell's frustration.

"You're all nuts!" He stomped over to the Dockers' table. "Let's go before they take all of your money."

The couple left their winnings behind and headed out the door with Mitchell.

The saloon erupted in noise, everyone talking at once. Bernie stuck his fingers in his mouth, whistled and then the place quieted.

"I don't know what you're up to, Destiny," a voice in the back called out. "Don't forget you represent everyone in Lizard Gulch, and some of us think we should sell out to Custer."

"I haven't forgotten who I represent," Destiny said. "My first priority is to make sure none of us gets ripped off."

"Are you really going to keep the Dockers' money and put it toward a drive-in?" Sonja asked.

"Looks like the majority of the town is here. I need one person to motion for a meeting," Destiny said.

Sonja raised her arm. "I motion we have a town meeting."

"I second that motion," Enrick said.

"Let's discuss the idea of putting bingo winnings toward town improvements."

"Like what?" Frank asked.

"What about a sewer system?" Bernie said. "Then we don't have to pay the Lil' Stinky man to pump out our septic tanks. That company keeps raising their rates."

"Or we could open a library."

"Or what about a museum?"

"Nothing needs to be decided today," Destiny said. "We'll put the money the Dockers won in a container and keep it here on the bar." She waved at Hank. "Maybe you can find a second jar for suggestions. If you have an idea on how to spend the money, put it in the jar," Destiny said. "The next meeting we'll vote on the suggestions."

"What if some of us don't want to donate our bingo winnings?" Violet asked.

"All in favor of collecting the bingo winnings and putting them toward town improvements raise your hand," Destiny said. Sixteen in favor—twelve against. She suspected even those who didn't want to give up their winnings would gladly do so to keep the money out of the Dockers' hands.

"Enjoy the rest of your night." She left the bar and Buck was right behind her. Neither said a word as they hopped on the bike and he drove them to the garage.

The silence continued as they climbed the stairs and entered the apartment. As soon as Buck shut the door, he spun Destiny and pressed her against the wall. His mouth hovered over hers. "Did I ever tell you that it turns me on when you get all mayorlike in front of the town?"

She took a deep breath but little oxygen got to her brain, leaving her dizzy. "I don't believe you have."

"You didn't ask for my vote," he said.

"What's your vote?" she whispered.

"I vote we do this…" His mouth closed over Destiny's, and all her troubles vanished.

She threaded her fingers through his hair and held his face. She wanted a real kiss and she wanted it now. Using her tongue she coaxed his mouth open and pressed herself against him. She felt the hard ridge of flesh beneath his jeans zipper and knew her fantasy was about to come true.

Chapter Nine

This was crazy, but Buck didn't want to stop.

He walked Destiny backward through the apartment—not an easy task with their lips locked together and their eyes closed. He'd fantasized about this moment since he'd first seen her dressed in white leather and a wedding veil.

He paused in front of the bedroom door and waited for her eyes to open. Her lashes fluttered up, and he caught a glimpse into her soul—those baby blues were begging him to make love to her. He dipped his head for another kiss but hesitated. He had to be sure.

"What's the matter?" Her words puffed against his chin. "Why did you stop?"

"Is this what you want?" Neither of them had said anything about how they felt about the other—at least not out loud. "I like you a lot, Destiny." She flinched. "Sorry, that didn't come out right." He held her hands. "I'm not sure what's happening between us. All I know is that being with you makes me feel good. Really good." She remained silent, and he struggled to convey his feelings without being dishonest. "I don't know what tomorrow will bring or what road I'll travel. All I can tell you—" *promise you* "—is that right here… right now…I'm exactly where I want to be."

"I want this, too, Buck."

There had been no hesitation on her part, and he lowered his head intent on kissing her, but she flattened her palms against his chest and pushed. "I need a minute in the bathroom."

After she shut the door, Buck willed his body to cool off—he didn't want to rush their lovemaking. He stepped outside and stared at a sunset most people only saw in the movies. Maybe an outdoor theater wasn't such a crazy idea. Before the show, couples could sit in their cars and watch the sky turn pink, purple and orange. There was no better ambience than a desert sunset for a date-night kiss.

A shuffling sound caught his attention and he turned. *Holy. Moly.*

Destiny was a goddess.

She stood in nothing but her birthday suit. She wore her hair loose—the long, fiery locks falling over her shoulders, concealing her breasts.

"Are you going to stay there or come here?"

He didn't need to be asked twice. He pulled Destiny into his arms. He ran his fingers down her spine, investigating the little notches in her vertebrae then he paid special attention to her neck. "You smell like honeysuckle and warm woman."

Rising on tiptoe, she pressed her mouth against his cheek and he felt her hot tongue lick his skin, setting it on fire. He groaned. "That's what I like most about you."

"What's that?" She nudged her pelvis against his arousal.

"You're uninhibited." *And you make me burn.* He nibbled the underside of her chin and skimmed his hands across her shoulders and down her arms. He avoided touching her breasts, wanting to slowly arouse her…make her yearn for him the way he longed for her. "I like that you're bold." He kissed the patch of skin behind her ear then inhaled her feminine scent. "I like that you're not afraid to take what you want."

Her hand found the hardness in his jeans. "I want."

"Not so fast." He moved her hand to his chest, pressing it over his heart. "I want to go slow." A woman like Destiny came along once in a man's lifetime—if he was lucky. Buck wasn't about to mess this up. He kissed a path along the curve of her shoulder then down her chest between her breasts.

Her moan emboldened him, and he lifted her against him, bringing her breasts even with his face. He growled, the noise rumbling through his chest and up his throat, where the sound vibrated against her skin. Her hands pressed his head closer, begging for more. He aimed to please.

Standing in the middle of the living room, Buck lost himself in the taste and feel of Destiny. Time slowed to a crawl and the only thing that registered in his mind was the rising testosterone level in his blood and an urgent need to feed his craving for the woman in his arms.

He swept Destiny off her feet and carried her into the bedroom. The heat they were generating would turn the place into a sauna in no time so he left the door open. He laid her on the bed then stared at her beautiful body, soaking in her sexiness…the need for him shining in her blue gaze.

She reached for him. "You have too many clothes on."

He tugged off his T-shirt and dropped it to the floor. "Loosen your belt, but don't take it off."

"Bossy little thing, aren't you?" He undid the buckle, letting the ends hang open. "Now what?"

"Unzip your jeans."

"Yes, ma'am." He did as instructed.

"Take off your boots."

He sat on the edge of the bed and removed his Ariats. He waited for the next command.

"Come closer," she whispered.

After he reclined next to her on the mattress, she slid her hands inside his jeans and cupped his backside. Destiny's boldness set Buck on edge and his heart pounded inside his chest. What if she'd been right—what if he couldn't handle her?

Her nails dug into his flesh, and he hissed. "Are you going to let me in on this fun?"

She giggled—the girlish sound at odds with the possessive gleam in her eyes. She shoved his jeans and briefs over his hips and down his thighs. There was no hiding what she did to him. He kicked off the pants then stretched out on top of her and took his dang sweet time familiarizing himself with her curves.

Her teeth nipped his shoulder. "Buck?"

Please don't tell me you changed your mind. "What?"

"Can we *not* go slow the first time?"

He stared into her eyes. "I was trying to—"

"I know." Her mouth curved into a wicked smile. "Right now, I really want—"

He cut her off with his lips and their kisses grew hotter and deeper. He tasted her desire…her need for him. Destiny was everything he never even knew he wanted…until now.

He sheathed himself then she guided him inside her. Forget slow and easy. Their lovemaking was as bold and forward as the woman in his arms, and without warning, she took Buck over the edge in a death-defying plunge he feared he'd never survive.

BUCK DIDN'T KNOW how much time had passed when he'd completed the journey back to consciousness…his body drained. Bracing himself, he peeked at the woman resting next to him on the bed.

Destiny was sound asleep.

He exhaled a quiet sigh. He hadn't had a clue what he should say to her after that incredible experience. Gently, so as not to disturb her, he caressed one of her curls between his fingers. She was like a stick of dynamite—all that power packed in a pretty package. When he'd lit her fuse, she'd exploded into a fireworks display so bright and beautiful she blinded him.

He recalled the few relationships with women he'd had in the past and none of the ladies had made him feel as alive in their arms as he'd felt with Destiny. When he gazed into her eyes he felt a surge of energy—as if *she* was the fuel he needed to run on.

The only reason you feel this way is because you got caught up in her and Lizard Gulch's problems and you've been on the road too long. Plus you're bored.

He'd been bored with his life long before he'd stirred things up with Will and had left the farm. Buck had been toying with the idea of opening his own auto repair shop for a couple of years but hadn't had the guts to make the move. Maybe he'd been waiting for the right motivation.

Was Destiny responsible for this sudden urge to move forward with his life and take control of his future?

Destiny rolled onto her side, facing Buck. Her mouth moved, forming silent words, and he wondered what she was dreaming about. Plenty of moonlight spilled through the bedroom window, illuminating Destiny's body. Their passion had exploded so quickly that he hadn't had a chance to see if she had any hidden tattoos. His gaze roamed over her limbs, then stalled on her hip. He touched the tip of his finger to the little red ladybug. A lizard, a flower and a ladybug—odd choices for a Harley girl, but he was getting used to the unexpected from Destiny.

When he considered her childhood, he couldn't help but admire her inner strength and stamina. Maybe they were a lot more alike than he'd first believed. Destiny appeared to have put her past behind her, refusing to follow in her mother's footsteps. And she'd found a place to call home and put down roots.

Buck had also moved on from the pain of growing up without a father. He and his brothers had talked about their fathers not being involved in their lives but when asked if he'd ever wanted to confront his—Buck had never felt the need. He believed he was better off not knowing the man.

He squeezed Destiny's hip and closed his eyes. If anything good had come of meeting her, it was that she'd given him the incentive to get his act together and make plans for his future. He'd talk to Troy about buying into his repair shop, and if his friend didn't want a partner, then Buck would make his own business plans.

As he listened to Destiny's gentle snoring, he wondered if she'd go into business with him. Lizard Gulch would never win the battle with Custer. Whether it happened a year from now or next month, the land developer would find a way to destroy the town and build his resort. Then where would Destiny go?

He smoothed his hand across her belly and her lashes fluttered—he hadn't meant to wake her, even though he wanted her again.

"How long have I been sleeping?"

"Long enough for me to enjoy admiring you." When he rubbed her stomach, she moved his hand to her breast, and he said, "This time we're not rushing." He kissed her neck, but she pushed him onto his back and climbed on top of him.

"I'm in the driver's seat."

"If I recall, you were driving last time." He chuckled. "When do I get a turn?"

"You will…eventually."

Talk ended, which was fine with Buck. Destiny's mouth was too distracting to have to keep track of conversation. He closed his eyes, his senses overwhelmed by her scent and touch. He could get used to her spoiling him with her brand of lovemaking. He'd let her have her way again, but next time she'd better watch out because he had a few things up his sleeve that even a Harley girl might find surprising.

DESTINY STARED AT the ceiling as the first rays of morning light filtered into the bedroom.

Don't you dare cry.

Eyes stinging, she willed the tears away. The last time she'd shed tears, she'd been seven and her mother had ruined the Christmas dress one of the truck stop waitresses had given her. Her mother had yanked on the sleeve to get Destiny's attention and had torn the material. It had been the last pretty dress she'd ever owned.

Buck's quiet snores drifted into her ear and she gathered the sound close to her heart. After waking up an hour ago and making love for the third time, he'd snuggled her against him and had fallen into a deep sleep, leaving her with too many thoughts racing through her head.

What an idiot she'd been—believing she could have sex with Buck and then send him on his way in a couple of weeks.

Don't be melodramatic. Been there. Done that. Big deal.

She wanted to curse the voice in her head and tell it to get lost, but that very voice had helped her survive in an environment no child should ever have to endure. And that same voice had left the truck stop with her, guiding her through close calls and sketchy experiences.

Maybe she was making a bigger deal out of this than she needed to. Buck was a big boy. She wasn't his first rodeo and he wasn't hers, although he was by far the best ride she'd ever had—that said a lot to a girl who owned a Wide Glide hog.

She snuggled against him, wondering why it was him and not some other guy who had to make her feel safe. Destiny had learned long ago to rely only on herself. If not for her toughness she'd be turning tricks in truck stops alongside her mother right now.

She wasn't sure why the Fates had brought Buck into her life after she'd become pregnant—when it would be impossible for them to be together. At least she'd have his memory to hold close to her heart the rest of her life. And because she didn't have many good memories, his would be all the more special.

He shifted on the mattress, sliding his thigh between her legs. His hand smoothed across her stomach, and she hoped he wouldn't wake up. After the first time they'd made love, she'd panicked when she'd felt his hand on her tummy, fearing he'd guess she was pregnant. She didn't want Buck to leave, knowing she was carrying another man's child—that's not how she wanted him to remember her.

And she didn't want him to think badly of her—being intimate so soon after being left pregnant at the altar. The truth was she'd never have slept with Daryl if he hadn't caught her on a bad day—the one-year anniversary of Simon Carter's death. She'd been in a funk all day when Daryl had stopped by the garage and suggested a night of dancing and drinking at the bars in Kingman. She'd woken the next morning in Daryl's bed with little memory of what had taken place in it.

Not long after that night the stick had turned blue, and she'd broken the news to Daryl that she was pregnant. He didn't offer to marry her. She'd asked him—for their baby's sake. Daryl had reluctantly agreed, and from that day on their friendship had cooled and they'd only had sporadic contact with each other—mostly texts and a couple of phone calls.

When Daryl had stopped in Lizard Gulch a few days ago, he'd apologized for ditching her at the altar but said he'd changed his mind and didn't want to get married because he didn't want the responsibility that went along with being a father. He did say he'd try to help her out financially whenever he could, but she didn't hold out much hope of receiving regular child-support checks from him.

Destiny wasn't angry with Daryl—she was glad he'd been honest with her. Now that she knew she couldn't count on him, she'd make different choices for her and the baby. The only demand she'd made of him was that he make an effort to visit their child. Daryl had agreed to try and had promised to keep Destiny informed of his whereabouts. It wasn't what she'd hoped for her child, but it was more than she'd had—at least the baby would know who his or her father was.

If only Buck had come into her life before that fateful night with Daryl—who knows, maybe she'd be carrying Buck's baby right now. No sense looking back—the only path was the one in front of her. Daryl was the least of her worries. If she wanted her child to grow up in one place, surrounded by people who cared, she had to find a way to save Lizard Gulch from the evil clutches of Custer.

"What's the matter? Why are you so tense?" Buck whispered, his lips moving against her arm.

Startled, Destiny stiffened. How long had Buck been awake? "I'm not tense."

"Then how come it feels like I'm cuddling a two-by-four?"

Destiny squirmed until she faced Buck. She brushed her hand over his heart and said, "I'm not used to sharing my bed."

"I'm glad." He peppered her face with kisses then captured her mouth in a bone-melting kiss that went on forever.

When Buck ended the kiss he tweaked her side and she giggled. "Stop, I'm ticklish."

"Really?" His fingers tormented her and Destiny begged for mercy. They made a mess of the bed, and in a desperate attempt to shield herself from his roving fingers, she snatched the blanket from the foot of the bed and covered herself.

"That won't stop me." He tickled the bottom of her foot and she shrieked.

"What the hell?"

Destiny and Buck froze then glanced in unison toward the doorway. Daryl stood bug-eyed with his mouth hanging open. The blanket protected her body from view but Buck wasn't so fortunate.

He reached for the sheet and flipped it across his waist. "Do you always enter a woman's apartment without knocking?"

Daryl didn't answer—probably because his mouth hung open.

"Get out, Daryl," she said.

Her command jarred Daryl out of his trance. "We need to talk." After he left the bedroom, she heard the door open and close.

"I thought it was over between you two." Buck watched her intently as if he believed he could read the truth in her eyes.

She sprang off the mattress then rummaged in the dresser drawer for a pair of panties. Buck remained in bed while she slipped on her underwear and a bra.

"Daryl and I are finished," she said. Shoot, they'd never even started.

"Then why is he at your apartment at the crack of dawn?"

"I don't know." She walked past the bed, but Buck snagged her wrist and tumbled her on top of him.

"If you have feelings for him, I want to know right

now. I don't make a habit of sleeping with another guy's lady."

"We're not together—not in the way you're implying."

"Okay." He released her and made a grab for his jeans. "I'll go out there and set good ol' Daryl straight."

"No." At his startled look she said, "I'll handle this." Buck put on his jeans then sat on the edge of the bed while she looked through the closet. After she dressed in a pair of shorts and a T-shirt, she fled the room.

"What do you want, Daryl?" she asked after she stepped outside.

"Sure didn't take you long to move on," he said.

"Skip the fake outrage. What do you want?"

"I came to tell you I got a new job."

"Where?"

"Sacramento."

"That's in California." He wouldn't see their child very often if he lived in another state.

"A friend's cousin got me a job as a bouncer at the bar out there. I'll make twice what I'm making in Kingman, so I can send you more money for the baby."

The thought was nice and she didn't doubt Daryl was sincere, but the old adage…out of sight out of mind, was probably closer to the truth, and eventually he'd forget about her and the baby.

Daryl's gaze cut to the door. "Does he know you're pregnant?"

"No, and it doesn't matter, because he's leaving town and I'll never see him again."

"Then it's not serious between you two?"

"This is just…" She waved a hand in the air. "Never mind."

Daryl's shoe hovered over the stairs. "I'm not leaving for another month."

"What's the name of the bar where you'll be working?"

"The Corner...I can't recall off the top of my head. Once I get there, I'll text you a phone number."

Daryl was lying—there was no new job. He was on the run.

At least he told you he was leaving. She wouldn't have to wonder what happened to him after months went by and he didn't call. "Do you want to know when the baby's born?"

"When's your due date?" he asked.

She'd told him a dozen times. "March."

"I'll call you."

"What about your mother? Do you want me to contact her about the baby?" If he did, she'd need his mother's number.

"I'll tell her," Daryl said.

There went the possibility of her child having a grandparent.

Your baby will have plenty of grandparents in Lizard Gulch.

Daryl peered past her shoulder and stiffened.

Great. Buck must be standing on the other side of the screen door. If she had any doubt, Buck put it to rest when he spoke.

"Everything okay out there?"

"Daryl got a new job in California."

"I'll be in touch." Daryl couldn't leave fast enough. As soon as his feet hit the gravel below, he hopped into his beater and took off, spewing dust in the air.

Chapter Ten

"Destiny, can I have a word with you, please?"

"I'll be right with you, Hank."

For the tenth time that morning, another resident of Lizard Gulch walked into the garage with a complaint about the Dockers. Buck was content to eavesdrop beneath Bernie's car while he worked on the undercarriage. The one time he'd pushed the creeper into the open, Harriet Wilson had unloaded on him, and he was just a guest in town.

Admit it. You like the idea that the old coots view you as one of their own now.

He did appreciate being treated as if he were a native son, but it irked him that Destiny was taking flack for something she had no control over. The townspeople should be turning their anger on Mitchell.

"I want Bernie to make the Dockers leave town, but he insists that he needs your permission," Hank said.

"What have the Dockers done?" Destiny asked.

"They won't pay their tab. I told them that I don't take credit cards. Now they're telling me they don't travel with cash and I need to get with the times and either install an ATM machine in the bar or accept credit cards."

"But you do take credit cards," Destiny said.

"Only from people I trust. I don't trust the Dockers."

Hank had taken Buck's debit card without blinking an eye. Obviously the bar owner trusted him.

"Have you mentioned this to the former mayor?" Destiny asked.

"Mitchell said it wasn't his problem."

"Don't serve the Dockers unless they pay cash upfront," Destiny said.

"I don't want them in my bar, period," Hank said. "If they get wind that Bernie's coming after them, maybe they'll take off."

"Bernie doesn't have the legal authority to make anyone do anything." Destiny's steel-toed boot tapped against the cement floor.

"What about keeping them under house arrest?" Hank asked. "Bernie could sit outside the motel and make sure they don't try to leave."

Buck shoved the creeper out from beneath the car and stood. "How's it going, Hank?"

"Could be better." The older man scowled.

Buck looked at Destiny. "I agree with Hank."

"About what?" she asked.

"The only reason Mitchell brought the Dockers here is to stir up trouble," Buck said. "Tell them if they don't pay their tab in cash they won't be welcome in town. Worst-case scenario…they take off in the middle of the night and you never see them again."

"Amen," Hank said.

"I'll speak to the Dockers about their bar tab." Destiny held up a finger in warning. "But we're not barricading them in their room."

"What about Bernie?" Hank said. "If he makes a

nuisance of himself, maybe the Dockers will get sick of him and pay me."

Destiny's shoulders slumped. "Tell Bernie he can keep an eye on the Dockers, but no verbal threats."

"Got it." Hank left Buck and Destiny alone in the garage.

An awkward silence settled between them. The day had begun on an uncomfortable note and hadn't improved since. It seemed like days ago, not hours, that good ol' Daryl had interrupted their morning after. Buck wanted to talk about last night—in his mind the experience had been incredible. And he'd sworn Destiny had enjoyed making love to him, but he'd learned a long time ago that the worst mistake a guy could make was assuming he knew what a woman was thinking— it always backfired on him.

You're feeling insecure.

What if he was?

"You okay?" His gaze dropped from her face to her outfit—a black formfitting tank top and cutoff jean shorts. His fingers itched to slide the strap off her shoulder and kiss the tan skin.

"I'm not worried about the Dockers."

He brushed at a loose strand of hair, peeking from beneath her ball cap. "I was referring to last night."

A pink tinge spread across her cheeks. "Oh." She pretended to straighten the tools on the workbench.

"You've been quiet." He worried her silence had nothing to do with their lovemaking and everything to do with Daryl.

"I'm tired."

He didn't doubt that. Neither of them had gotten much sleep last night. He didn't want to push her if she wasn't ready to talk, but he feared she was having second thoughts about Daryl after he announced he was moving to California. "If you're sure."

"I'm sure."

He'd taken a chance when he'd slept with Destiny so soon after she'd been left at the altar, and he knew he might be the rebound guy. He was okay with that, because he was certain that with time she'd realize that he was a better catch than Daryl. But Daryl dropping the bomb that he was leaving the area had definitely affected Destiny. Some guys didn't want to be in a committed relationship, but they also didn't want the woman they left to move on and be happy with someone else. Buck couldn't figure out if Daryl fell into that category or not, and Destiny wasn't making it easy for him to guess how she felt about the situation.

"Are you okay?" she asked.

He grinned.

"What?"

"I've never had a woman ask me that before."

She shrugged. "Let's not make it into anything more than it is."

A sharp pain gripped his gut. That wasn't what he wanted to hear. "What do you think it was?" As soon as he asked the question, he regretted it. Now she'd assume he needed reassurance.

Her gaze locked on the Peg-Board above the bench, and her silence hurt.

"I'm cool with leaving it as it is...if that's what you want." He wanted more. He wasn't sure what *more* constituted—he just knew that he didn't want his time with Destiny to be a series of one-night stands.

He tugged on the brim of her cap until she made eye

contact with him. "I'm not trying to pressure you." He rubbed his thumb over her cheek. "But I want you to know that I don't fall into bed with every woman I meet. I like you, Destiny." He swallowed hard and went out on a limb. "I like you a lot."

Tears welled up in her eyes, and Buck's heart slammed against his rib cage. Usually when he told a girl that he liked her, she'd smile or kiss him. She sure as heck didn't cry.

"Destiny? Where are you?"

They both jumped at the question that preceded Mitchell into the garage.

"What do you want?" The scam artist annoyed Buck to no end.

"A word with Destiny."

Destiny turned her back to Mitchell and discreetly rubbed her eyes. "I'm listening."

"What's this I hear about you siccing Bernie on the Dockers until they pay their bar tab?"

"I didn't sic Bernie on anyone," she said.

"Then why did the Dockers find him sitting outside their motel room a few minutes ago?"

"Maybe Bernie's being friendly," Buck said.

Mitchell glared. "I didn't ask you."

"Hank said the Dockers refused to pay their tab with cash. Is that true?" Destiny asked.

"Hank has a credit-card machine. There's no reason he can't take the Dockers' card."

"You know he doesn't accept credit cards from strangers. You should have warned your friends." Destiny crossed her arms over her chest. "But you didn't. I wonder why?"

Mitchell pointed his finger. "I don't like what you're accusing me of."

"And what's that?" Buck wasn't about to be left out of the conversation.

"The Dockers have every right to be in Lizard Gulch. This is America. People can come and go where they want."

"Sure seems suspicious that a wealthy couple from Philadelphia would build a second home in a run-down desert town with few amenities." Buck quirked an eyebrow. "Unless they were getting paid to hang out in Lizard Gulch and pretend they wanted to move here."

"They haven't been bribed." Mitchell's gaze swung between Buck and Destiny. "Isn't it about time Buck Owens Cash went back to wherever it is country-and-western impersonators live?"

Reining in his temper, Buck said, "Destiny, give us a minute."

"Sure."

Buck waited until she crossed the street then faced off with Mitchell. "Don't underestimate these people. They're not stupid. They know what you're trying to do."

"I never said they were stupid, just helpless. They're finding out that the world is ruled by money and power."

"What about morality?" Buck said. "Got any of that in your world?"

"Don't act all sanctimonious. This town was destined to die eventually. At least I've negotiated a payout with Custer so they don't walk away with nothing."

Astonished, Buck said, "You really believe you're the good guy in all this?"

"Hell, yes. You don't see Destiny fighting to get the old people more money, do you?"

"You mean Melba, Hank, Enrick and Frank. They're the only ones getting paid if Custer takes this town. The rest will be left in the dust—literally."

"That's not my problem," Mitchell said.

"How long have you been doing this?"

"Doing what?"

"Destroying peoples' lives."

"My job is to make the wealthy wealthier. You can't accomplish that without some collateral damage." Mitchell walked off, ending the conversation.

If there was one thing Buck hated, it was a bully, and the only way to fight Mitchell and Custer was with a lawyer—one as cunning and cutthroat as the two businessmen. But there was a problem—the town couldn't afford a lawyer. *What about a fund-raiser?*

A lightbulb went off in Buck's head. He pulled his cell phone from his pocket and called his brother Mack and got his voice mail. "Mack, it's me, Buck. I need your help."

After leaving a detailed message, he went upstairs to Destiny's apartment and scrolled through his list of contacts then began reaching out to his rodeo buddies. Once he had a head count of guys willing to ride for nothing to raise money for Lizard Gulch, he called P. T. Lewis, a stock contractor who owned a ranch between Stagecoach and Yuma.

There was nothing like a rodeo, a free concert and a good cause to bring country folk together. Buck's gaze shifted to the bedroom door.

And he knew just how to persuade the mayor to go along with his plans.

"YOU'RE A DIFFICULT woman to pin down."

Destiny spun and came face-to-face with Buck. *Darn.* A week had passed since they'd slept together, and she'd done her best to avoid being alone with him—except at the end of the day when they retired to her apartment above the garage. And once the bedroom door shut, there had been no need for talk. After they made love, she promptly fell asleep in his arms, and when morning arrived, she sneaked out and worked on Bernie's car before Buck had crawled from bed.

"Do you always play a round of mini golf in the dark?" he asked.

"Sometimes."

Technically the sun had set an hour ago, but the lights from the pastry shop, Lucille's and Bernie's trailer along with the stars in the sky illuminated the putt-putt course well enough to see.

"Mind if I play with you?"

"Sure." There went her time to think. Reflect. And panic. While Buck fetched a rusty putter and a golf ball from the vacant concession stand, Destiny returned to the first hole and sat on the head of a miniature allosaurus.

When Buck joined her, he said, "You've been avoiding me."

Guilty. She enjoyed being with Buck—that's why she couldn't allow herself to become too attached to him. "You never mention when you plan to leave Lizard Gulch."

"Are you getting tired of me?" he whispered in her ear.

She'd never tire of him. "I figured you'd miss your

family or rodeo by now." She looked him in the eye. "Maybe even working with your mechanic friend." He couldn't help her in her garage forever.

"I miss my family, but I'll be seeing them soon."

Her heart dropped into her stomach.

You knew this day would come. Shoot, you've been pushing him away ever since you made love the first time.

In her defense, Buck was the first person since Simon and Sylvia Carter that she'd allowed to get close to her. "When are you leaving?" She set her ball on ground.

"I'm not leaving. My family is coming here."

The news jarred her, and she swung the club too hard, driving the ball like a missile toward the cave at the end of the green turf. The ball sailed into the opening, banged off the plaster wall and bounced out, rolling the length of the green until it hit Buck's boot and came to a stop.

"Nice shot," he said.

"What do you mean your family is coming to Lizard Gulch?"

"I didn't want to say anything until I knew all the details, but my brother's country-and-western band agreed to play a free concert after the rodeo."

"What rodeo?" When had he done all this?

"The only way you'll save the town, Destiny, is to fight Custer in court. To do that you need a lawyer."

"Lizard Gulch doesn't have the funds to pay for a lawyer."

"I know." He swung his club, sending the ball slow and steady toward the cave. It stopped an inch from the hole. "That's why I came up with the idea of a fund-raiser. The money collected from the rodeo and concert will pay the lawyer's fees."

Was he crazy? "Lizard Gulch is off the beaten path. Who'll come to a rodeo way out here?"

"My buddies on the circuit are spreading the word, and my sister made up flyers and posted them in Yuma and Stagecoach," Buck said. "The stock contractor providing the animals for the rodeo is using his connections to promote the event. Rodeo cowboys and their fans are a tight group, Destiny. You'll see on Saturday."

"This coming Saturday?"

"Yep."

That was three days from now. She didn't know whether to hug Buck or haul off and sucker punch him. "Does anyone else know about this?"

He shook his head. "I thought you should be the one to break the news."

Destiny wanted to resent Buck for taking charge of a problem that was hers to solve, but she was grateful he was trying to help. She followed him to his ball. "What's in it for you?"

"What do you mean?"

"Why would you care about helping this town when you don't live here?"

"I care about you." Buck brushed his knuckles across her cheek, and she almost melted against him. "And I don't like bullies," he said.

She felt as if she'd let her constituents down, because she'd assumed the town couldn't afford a lawyer. She should have made a few calls and found out for sure. "How can I help?"

"We'll need to order several Porta Potties and have enough food and beer on hand to feed the crowd."

She motioned to his golf ball. "Mind if we finish this game later? We have a lot to accomplish in three days, so I'd better call a town meeting tonight." She placed her ball and putter in the empty shack. "I wish you'd have told me this sooner."

"I would have if you hadn't been avoiding me and then—" he snagged her arm "—at night, I couldn't think of anything but you after we went to bed."

She saw it coming—his mouth. The light caress of his lips, testing her response before he thrust his tongue inside. She inched closer and gave in to the need that was always present whenever Buck touched her.

"Hate to break up a romantic kiss, but Hank sent me to get you." Enrick stood at the entrance to the course.

She broke free from Buck's embrace. "What's the matter?"

"Mitchell's stirring up trouble."

Buck walked behind the pair. "What's he doing now?"

"Threatening to call the police on Bernie, if he doesn't stop stalking the Dockers."

Destiny entered Lucille's and took in the chaos. A fight had broken out between Mitchell and Bernie, and by the looks of it both men could use a few pointers on brawling.

"Stop!" Destiny charged forward, grabbed Bernie by the back of his shirt and yanked him off Mitchell.

"He started it!" Bernie spat.

Mitchell smoothed his messy hair into place then tucked his dress shirt into his pants.

"You ought to be ashamed of yourself, Mark—" Destiny stomped her foot "—fighting an old man."

"You're worried about him?" Mitchell pushed his shirtsleeve up, revealing bite marks. "He tried to gnaw off my arm!"

Aware the room was divided—half standing with the former mayor and the other half supporting the sheriff, Destiny said, "Everyone sit down." When no one moved, she shouted, "Now!"

Feet shuffled as the crowd settled at the various tables. Once the mumbling and grumbling quieted, she walked to the front of the room. "Bernie, I don't think there's one person here who doesn't admire your loyalty to this town, but from now on you stay away from the Dockers."

"But—"

"If you don't, I'll take your badge."

Bernie's mouth dropped open.

"Quit the dramatics," Mitchell said. "It's not even a real badge."

Bernie shoved his chair back, but Destiny pinned him with a dark look and he remained seated.

She faced Mitchell. "You are no longer the mayor. You were recalled, because the people of Lizard Gulch could no longer trust you." At least he had the grace to look embarrassed. "I'm ordering you to stop intimidating and harassing people. If you don't, I'll file a report with the Kingman police department."

Mitchell fisted his hands. "You wouldn't dare."

"Try me."

Seconds ticked off on the clock on the wall, but finally he backed down. Honestly, she didn't know why he made the drive to and from Kingman every day to hang out in town when he harbored such disdain for its residents.

"We've got a lot of work to do in the next three days, and it's going to require everyone's help," she said.

The door opened and the Dockers walked in. They stopped suddenly when they noticed the large gathering. "Sorry," Jim said. "We didn't mean to intrude." The couple backpedaled.

"Stay." Destiny waited until they sat down.

"What's going on?" Sonja asked from the back of the room.

"With Buck's help, the town is hosting a rodeo and a music concert this Saturday."

No one said a word. "The money we raise from the event will pay a lawyer to represent us against Wyndell Resorts and—" Destiny nodded "—Mr. Mitchell's activities."

"No lawyer will help this town, because you don't have a case." Mitchell laughed.

"I believe we do," she said. "And if we don't, then you won't have to worry, will you?"

"Does this mean Delores and I came here for nothing?" Jim asked.

Mitchell gave the signal for Jim to hold his tongue.

"This is a great chance to bring in new business for the saloon and the pastry shop. We'll need volunteers to spruce up the town and create a welcome sign out by the highway."

"I'll do it!" Sonja shoved her hand in the air.

"How many folks you think will be coming?" Frank spoke up.

Destiny looked at Buck, and he said, "A couple hundred at least."

"I'd better call for a liquor delivery." Hank disappeared into the kitchen.

"We'll need a place to hold the rough stock," Destiny said. "Any suggestions?"

"Put the bulls in the cemetery," Bernie said.

"What about Maisy?" Melba ignored Mitchell's laugh. "Won't she be upset if the graves are trampled?"

"Serves her right for terrorizing people," Delores grumbled.

"Did Maisy visit you in your motel room?" Bernie asked the Dockers.

"She won't leave us alone," Delores said.

Destiny caught Buck's grin, but took charge of the conversation before folks got sidetracked swapping ghost stories. "What about the horses?"

"No need to worry about the rough stock," Buck said. "The rodeo production company will bring temporary holding pens."

Destiny could only imagine the smell in town by the time the rodeo left. "Where should the band set up for the concert?"

"In back of the motel," Melba said. "They can put their stage at the end of the pool. That way folks can swim or sit on the grass and listen to the music."

"So we're all on board with this?" Destiny asked one last time.

"What if we're not?" Bob Wilson stepped from the shadows. "What if some of us don't want our town invaded by a rodeo or a bunch of rock and roll freaks?"

"It's a country-and-western band, and if they don't

invade us and help raise money, then you won't have a town to complain about, Mr. Wilson."

When the old man remained quiet, Destiny said, "Those of you who oppose the rodeo and concert won't have to help of course, but I'd advise you to find somewhere else to be this Saturday, because Lizard Gulch is going to turn into a Wild West town for one day."

Chapter Eleven

"Ladies and gents, hang on to your hats for the final event of the afternoon. It's time for a little bull poker!" A roar echoed through the bleachers, bringing a smile to Destiny's face. She was thrilled that all the town's residents had turned out for the rodeo—even those leaning toward taking the buyout from Custer.

When she'd explained the reason for the fund-raiser, everyone had agreed that no matter what happened in the end—whether Wyndell Resorts claimed the town or not—they'd need a lawyer to make sure Custer played fair.

Destiny swung her gaze to the men gathering near the bull chute. Buck and his siblings were easy to pick out among the others—the Cash brothers were the best-looking cowboys here. Not only were the six brothers handsome and full of swagger, but they were talented. Buck and Will had won the tie-down roping event then Mack and Conway had ridden in the saddle-bronc competition and took first and third places. Johnny rode in the bareback event and had come in second. Porter had been the only Cash brother crazy enough to compete in bull riding. Although he'd been tossed after two seconds, the buckle bunnies in the crowd had gone crazy, acting as if he'd won a national championship.

The rodeo had begun three hours ago, and Destiny had been amazed at how quickly the event had come together. P. T. Lewis and his crew had arrived before dawn and set up the bleachers, the arena and the temporary corrals for the livestock. By the time folks had crawled out of bed, the town had been transformed into a rodeo venue.

"Do we have four brave men willing to play a hand of poker?" the announcer asked.

"I hope Buck doesn't volunteer." Destiny spoke out loud.

"Don't worry…the bull's harmless." Buck's sister Dixie spoke. "He's a family pet."

The bull in the chute bellowed as if it didn't appreciate being described as harmless. Destiny's gut twisted but not from morning sickness. Her queasy stomach had disappeared a week ago, leaving her with an insatiable appetite, which was being teased by the scent of barbecue cooking in the smokers behind Lucille's.

"Dixie and I have practiced on Curly several times in the past," Shannon said. The former female rough stock rider was married to Buck's eldest brother, Johnny.

"I can't believe you rode bulls." Destiny considered herself a tough chick, but even she wasn't crazy enough to hop on the back of a bull.

Shannon's green eyes sparkled as she adjusted her sleeping baby girl in her arms. "And I loved every second of it—even the times I got dumped in the dirt."

"I envy you," Will's wife, Marsha, said. "I've never done anything that daring in my whole life."

"Yes, you have." Dixie's eyes twinkled and Marsha blushed. "You married my brother."

Before the Cash clan had arrived, Buck had given Destiny the rundown on his family. Marsha was the daughter of a local pastor—she'd slept with Will the night of their prom and ended up pregnant. Will had asked her to get an abortion and believed she had done so before she'd gone off to college in California. Buck said Marsha had kept the baby and raised their son on her own the past fourteen years—until this summer when she'd returned to Stagecoach and informed Will he had a son. Now Marsha and Will were married, and the new family appeared to be happy.

Destiny would love to talk to Marsha about her pregnancy and fear of being a single parent, but she didn't dare. The Cash family was a tight-knit group and she didn't trust Marsha not to tell her husband. When Buck left Lizard Gulch, Destiny wanted his last memory of her to be what they'd shared and not the fact that she'd hid her pregnancy from him.

"The other day Javier and Miguel told Conway that they want to grow up and be rodeo cowboys," Conway's wife, Isi, said. "I'm not sure my heart would survive the stress."

Destiny pressed her hand against her stomach. Isi had married Conway after they'd been friends for a couple of years. Buck claimed Conway never wanted children, but after watching Isi's twin sons for several weeks, he'd grown attached to the boys and had fallen in love with Isi. Was it possible Destiny might one day find her own happy ever after like the Cash women?

"You'll have more than rodeoing to worry about with

the twins, Isi," Dixie said. "Javi and Mig are going to be drop-dead gorgeous when they grow up. Your phone will ring off the hook with fathers warning your sons away from their daughters."

The women laughed.

"Looks like we've got our four poker players," the announcer said.

Applause rippled through the stands while a pair of cowboys set up a card table and chairs in the middle of the arena.

"How 'bout a warm welcome to the first fool of the bunch, Bernie Flynn, from right here in Lizard Gulch."

Bernie? The old fart was going to get himself killed. He sat down in the chair facing the bull chute, and Destiny debated whether or not to walk into the arena and drag his carcass out of there.

"The next crazy wannabe cowboy is Mark Mitchell from Phoenix."

This could be interesting... She'd love it if Curly tossed the arrogant lawyer on his ass. Mitchell sat in the chair on Bernie's left.

"Well, now I don't believe my eyes. Looks like we got a cowgirl brave enough to face down a bull."

The stands exploded with shouts and cheers as Melba pranced into the arena, waving a pink silk scarf. "I sure hope you're right about Curly, Shannon," Destiny said.

"Our last dummy is Buck Owens Cash!"

Whoever ran the sound system cranked the volume and the song "All Around Cowboy" by Buck Owens blared from the speakers. The fans went wild, and Destiny gaped at the females in front of her who whistled and preened when Buck waved his cowboy hat at them.

A jealous urge to shout at the women that Buck was hers almost drove her to her feet.

"Don't pay attention to them," Dixie whispered in Destiny's ear. "Buck only has eyes for you."

Destiny was embarrassed that Buck's sister had seen through her. It must be pregnancy hormones that made it impossible to hide her feelings. "We're just friends."

Dixie laughed. "That's what my brothers all say when they fall in love with a woman."

Fall in love? Buck didn't love her. Did he?

As if Dixie had read her thoughts, she whispered, "Buck hasn't come right out and said as much, but it's there in his eyes when he looks at you." She tilted her head toward the arena. "Like now."

The air in Destiny's lungs seeped out in a quiet puff of air. Buck stopped in front of the stands where Destiny sat and placed his hat against his chest then bowed. Her heart melted at the gesture and she blew him a kiss.

"Looks like Buck Owens Cash has a lady he'd like to impress this afternoon. Let's see if he's the last man sitting when the bull charges." The announcer cranked up the Buck Owens music while Buck took the only empty chair at the table and sat with his back to the chute.

"Ladies and gents, are you ready?"

The crowd stomped their boots on the bleachers and chanted "Let Curly loose!"

The gate opened and the bull walked into the arena as if he was out for a Sunday stroll. The fans hooted and hollered when a rodeo clown hopped over the rails and waved his hat in the bull's face, hoping to ignite a fire under the animal's hooves. Curly would have none of it. He meandered over to the table then bellowed at the poker players who held cards in their hands and pretended the bull was no threat.

When Curly inched closer, all the players except Buck placed their cards facedown and sat forward in their chair prepared to sprint to safety.

"It's all part of the show," Shannon said. "Curly won't charge. P.T.'s granddaughter pretty much tamed him and now he won't hurt a flea."

"Thank goodness," Destiny said. She'd hate for Buck, Melba or Bernie to get hurt. She couldn't care less about Mitchell.

Shouts from the stands grew louder as Curly walked closer. None of players bolted, not even Melba. Then Curly changed directions and closed in on Mitchell. When Curly got within arm's reach, the lawyer chickened out and ran for safety.

Destiny expected Curly to give chase, but the bull only head-butted the vacated chair, tossing it into the air. The crowd jeered Mitchell, taunting him for being a coward—served the braggart right.

"We got two cowboys and a cowgirl left," the announcer said. "You might think Curly's not a threat, but you can never tell when a bull gets it into his head to go on a rampage."

Curly walked over to Melba's chair. Despite Shannon's assurances that the bull wouldn't harm anyone, Destiny held her breath along with everyone in the stands. When Curly stuck his head in Melba's face she smacked his nose with her cards, and the bull backed up and bawled.

"Would you look at that." The announcer chuckled. "Not even a bull gets away with taunting a determined woman."

Applause and catcalls echoed through the air as Curly stood docile, swishing his tail. Destiny wondered if this would be the end of the poker game when the bull pawed the ground. Bernie's mouth dropped open at the plume of dust rising into the air. Curly bent his head and that was all the encouragement Bernie needed—he shoved his chair back and ran for safety.

"Down to two players, folks. Who's it gonna be— the cowboy or the cowgirl?"

The announcer had barely finished his spiel when Curly dropped his head and rammed the table, sending the poker cards sailing through the air. The crowd yelled encouragement—others, like Destiny, shouted warnings.

"Run, Melba!" The motel owner was a tough bird, but she couldn't hold her own against a bull—not even a friendly one.

Melba leaned over and whispered into Buck's ear then scurried away, her pink scarf forgotten. Buck and Curly faced off, the bull stomping his front hoof on the ground and snorting. Buck stared Curly down.

"I think we got ourselves a winner, folks! Buck Owens Cash!"

Destiny didn't care that Buck won the poker challenge— she wanted him safe and the heck away from Curly.

Buck waved his hat to the crowd then patted the bull on the rump and walked off, man's best friend dogging his boot heels. Johnny met Buck at the gate, tossed a rope over Curly's head then led the bull out of the arena and over to the cemetery, where Curly lay down in the shade beneath the hanging tree.

"I hope all you ladies and gents enjoyed today's rodeo," the announcer said. "The Cowboy Rebels concert begins in an hour, so make sure you fill up on barbecue before you head over to the Flamingo Motel."

"I don't know about you girls," Shannon said, "but I'm sitting in one of the rocking chairs on the porch of that pastry shop until the food line dwindles."

"I'll go with you," Dixie said.

"I better corral the boys before they get into trouble." Isi walked off in search of Conway and the twins.

"If I know Ryan and Will, they're already in line for barbecue." Marsha joined the crowd moving up the street to Lucille's.

Left alone, Destiny relaxed for the first time in hours. She liked Buck's family, but she worried that they'd assume she and Buck were more than… *What?*

Hoping to avoid an argument with herself, she left the bleachers and went in search of her cowboy.

"Looking for me?" Grinning, Buck opened his arms and without any hesitation Destiny walked into them. Why did this have to feel so right? Why did Buck have to be the one who made her heart pound? A lump grew in her throat when she thought of never seeing him again.

"You hungry?" he asked.

You have no idea. She skimmed her hand through his hair, knocking his hat to the ground then she lifted her mouth to his. Whistles rent the air, but Destiny didn't hear them over the thumping of her heart and the whirring sound of blood racing through her veins. After she thoroughly kissed Buck and assured herself that he was okay, she released him. "Don't you ever play bull poker again."

"Yes, ma'am." Buck grasped her hand and led her over to his brothers.

Aside from Johnny, who had dark hair and blue eyes, the rest of the Cash brothers had brown eyes and brown hair with varying shades of blond and gold highlights.

"What did you think of the rodeo, Destiny?" Mack asked.

"It was great, and if your singing voice is anything like your talking voice then the concert will be pretty darn good, too."

Mack poked Buck in the shoulder. "Keep her. She'll liven up things at the farm."

"Buck says you own a Wide Glide hog." Porter flashed a smile that Destiny was positive had made hundreds of girls swoon.

"I do." The brothers exchanged glances. Then she caught Buck grinning. "I'm guessing all of you want to take my hog for a spin."

"Destiny," Will said, "I wouldn't trust anyone but me with your bike. I owned a Harley in high school and—"

"It might have been a Harley but it was a piece of crap," Buck said.

"Crap or not, it was a Harley." Will shoved Buck playfully.

Destiny stood silent, amused by the brothers' antics. *This is what it's like to be part of a big family.* She hated the idea that her child would grow up lonely with just her for family. "All of you can take turns on my bike, but if I find one scratch or dent, then you're buying me a new hog." She tossed the keys to Buck before she walked off. She hadn't even made it to the street when she heard one of the brothers speak.

"Never in a million years would I have pictured you with a girl like Destiny."

She slowed her pace, but one of the bulls in the cemetery bawled, drowning out Buck's response.

Probably for the best.

"THAT WAS A decent rodeo," Custer said, stepping outside of Lucille's. Buck had invited the man to the rodeo and concert, hoping to convince him to embrace his idea to save the town and give both sides what they wanted.

"P. T. Lewis has been in the rodeo production business for two decades," Buck said. "He knows how to entertain folks."

"Where is everyone?" Custer asked.

"At the Flamingo. The concert begins in a few minutes."

"Concert?" Custer's eyebrows rose. "You thought of everything."

"Have you had time to consider my suggestion?" Buck asked.

"It's ballsy—I'll give you that, Cash."

"Hey, I've been looking all over for you!" Mark Mitchell waved from the pastry shop steps. He shoved what was left of his doughnut into his mouth then hurried across the street. "What's going on?" he asked.

Buck ignored Mitchell and spoke to Custer. "If you keep the town and build the resort next to it, you'll have a unique attraction for your guests right in your backyard."

"What the hell are you talking about?" Mitchell gaped at Buck.

Custer motioned for his sidekick to shut up. "Let the man speak."

"You're out in the middle of nowhere." Buck spread his arms wide. "After a few days of golf and spa treatments the guests will grow bored and want to leave. If you include Lizard Gulch as part of the resort, guests will have more to do. Kids can play miniature golf or swim in the motel pool. People can take ghost tours at night. If one of the guests's vehicles breaks down, there's an auto mechanic on-site."

Buck ignored Mitchell's derisive grunt and continued his push. "The town might seem hokey to you, but this place is a Route 66 gem. It's got character and characters who live here. If you want to make a big impression on your guests and have them spread the word about your resort, then you keep Lizard Gulch right where it is."

"I'd have to put money into the town. Spruce it up a bit," Custer said, eyeing the unpaved street.

"You're kidding, right?" Mitchell frowned. "You're not considering his stupid idea, are you? The people here are crazy. They'll scare the resort guests away."

"Watch your mouth, Mitchell. The old folks are eccentric but they're harmless." Buck pointed to the two towering palm trees guarding the entrance to the motel and the neon sign in the shape of a giant flamingo. "The Flamingo has historic value. If word spreads that you're trying to save a Route 66 landmark, people will want to give you their business. If they find out you want to destroy a part of America's history, then they'll boycott your resort and spend their money elsewhere."

"What's in it for you, Cash?" Custer asked. "Why do you care what happens to this desert dump?"

"He cares because he's sleeping with the town mechanic," Mitchell said.

Buck cared because he identified with these people. A kid didn't grow up the son of a vamp and carry the moniker of Buck Owens Cash without having experienced his share of mockery and teasing. "The people who call Lizard Gulch home might be society misfits in your eyes, but they're a family." An odd family, but a family nonetheless. "You bulldoze this town and they'll scatter to the four corners. At their age they might never see each other again."

"He's crazy, Jack." Mitchell stomped his foot like a little boy. "You offer the old farts money to relocate their trailers and they'll be out of your hair in less than twenty-four hours."

"That plan won't work after today's fund-raiser," Buck said.

"Fund-raiser for what?" Custer asked.

"To raise money to retain a lawyer to represent Lizard Gulch in a counter lawsuit against Wyndell Resorts."

"You don't say?" Custer grinned.

"What the hell is so funny?" Mitchell asked.

"I've never been sued by a town before."

"Don't underestimate Destiny," Buck said. "She's a fighter and she'll go down swinging."

"Who cares, as long as she goes down," Mitchell said.

"If Destiny fails—" Buck stuck his face into Mitchell's "—you can bet you'll fail, too."

"Is that a threat, Cash?" Mitchell asked.

"A warning. Word travels fast in the desert, and rural people stick together. If you swindle these people, your reputation as a lawyer will be ruined."

Seconds ticked by, then Custer said, "I'll speak to my team about your idea."

"Don't take too long. The lawyer representing Lizard

Gulch isn't being paid to twiddle his thumbs." Buck kept a straight face when he told the lie. Custer and Mitchell didn't need to know Destiny hadn't hired a lawyer yet.

"Don't worry. I got your message loud and clear." Custer turned to his henchman. "I'm not ready to take a town vote to sell out just yet, so you'll have to stick around here until I decide what my next move will be."

The three men crossed the street just as Destiny walked through the motel parking lot. When she spotted Buck, her eyes rounded with shock.

Worried that she'd misinterpreted his chat with Custer and Mitchell, he hurried toward her. "Destiny, wait!" She turned her back and disappeared into the crowd.

"Buck, wait up!"

He stopped when Dixie called out his name. Custer and Mitchell continued to the motel without him. Irritated that he lost sight of Destiny, he grumbled, "I can't talk right now."

"You're grouchy," Dixie said. "What's the matter?"

"Nothing. Where's Nate?" He wasn't used to seeing his sister without his nephew in her arms.

"Gavin's watching him."

Buck resumed walking toward the motel. He ought to be able to spot Destiny—her red locks would stand out among all the blond-haired rodeo groupies.

"What's the hurry?" Dixie hustled along with him.

Buck slowed his steps. "What do you want, Dix?"

"I wanted to tell you we approve of Destiny."

He scanned the sea of heads. "Who's *we?*"

"Me and the other Cash wives."

"Since when does the woman I date need an endorsement from all the females in the family?"

"Destiny's on the quiet side and didn't talk about her family, but that doesn't matter."

"That's good to know." What would his sister and sisters-in-law think of Destiny if they knew she'd been raised in truck stops by a mother who turned tricks for a living?

Dixie snagged his shirtsleeve. "How serious are things between you two?"

Pretty damn serious—at least in Buck's mind. "I'm not sharing any pillow talk stories with you, Dix." He squirmed beneath her sharp stare.

"There's trouble in paradise, isn't there?" she said.

Possibly. He'd promised Destiny he wouldn't get involved in the town's problems, but he'd interfered anyway. He wouldn't be much of a man if he'd stood by and watched Custer and Mitchell work Destiny over like a prizefighter's punching bag. "We're fine."

"Then invite Destiny to the farm. Bring her to Stagecoach in two weeks and we'll plan a family picnic."

The last thing he wanted to do was parade Destiny in front of his family without knowing where things stood between them. "I'll think about it."

"Good. Now go find your Juliet. I'm going to look for my Romeo." Dixie walked off.

Buck pushed through the mass of people and made his way to the pool, where a stage had been set up next to the deep end. Mack and his bandmates were tuning their guitars and testing the sound system. Already a group of pretty girls had gathered by the stage, flirting with the Cowboy Rebels. He wondered if any of the girls were aware that the only single cowboy in the band was Mack.

"Hey, where have you been?" Johnny asked, approaching with the rest of Buck's brothers.

"I had some business to take care of," he said. "How'd you all manage to ditch your kids?"

"The twins are taking a nap and Isi's resting with them." Conway frowned. "She's been tired and cranky lately. Don't know what's gotten into her."

"Shannon's worried the music will hurt Addy's ears so she's going to sit in the truck bed in the parking lot and listen to the concert." Johnny shrugged. "Can't figure that woman out. She doesn't want our daughter's hearing damaged, but she's already planning out Addy's mutton bustin' career."

"Ryan's old enough to hang out by himself." Will motioned to his teen son, talking to a man wearing a beret, plaid shorts and a tank top. "Did you know that old guy was a research scientist for Procter & Gamble?"

"Really?" Buck said.

"Ryan's asking him about grad programs." Will frowned. "If I let him, he'd head off to college right now."

Buck hurt for Will. His brother had missed out on the first fourteen years of his son's life, and he doubted Will wanted Ryan to leave home any day soon.

"Who's watching Bandit while you guys are up here?" The black Lab had been left behind.

"Troy's got him out at his place," Conway said. "By the way, Troy keeps bugging me about when you're coming back. He said if you don't show up soon, he's going to replace you."

"I'll call him in a few days." Buck's first priority was making sure Destiny didn't think he'd betrayed her. If he couldn't convince her that he'd had the town's best interests at heart when he'd contacted Custer, then he might be asking Troy for his old job back.

Chapter Twelve

"Howdy, folks." Mack Cash tipped his cowboy hat to the crowd gathered around the pool and spilling into the motel parking lot. "I want to thank everyone for driving out to Lizard Gulch today and showing your support for this town."

Shouts, whistles and applause rippled through the evening air.

"For those of you who don't know us...we're the Cowboy Rebels." He played a few notes on his guitar, and the rodeo groupies danced in front of the stage.

Buck shared an amused look with Johnny. The girls sure loved their brother's deep voice. The band members were introduced and each cowboy played a solo, then Mack asked, "We got any line dancers here tonight?"

Several people raised their hands.

"I'm counting on you pretty girls up front to teach the others—" he strummed his guitar "—'Honky Tonk Badonkadonk'!" The band kicked off the song by Trace Adkins, and the ladies formed a line alongside the pool and strutted their stuff. Before long the locals and other guests joined in.

Buck searched for Destiny among the dancers but saw no sign of her. Maybe she'd gone back to the garage. He weaved through the bodies and almost made it to the parking lot when Mitchell stepped into his path.

The former mayor was getting on his nerves. "What do you want?" he shouted over the music.

Mitchell poked Buck's chest with his finger. "Mind your own business."

"Are you threatening me?"

"This isn't your town, Cash. You don't belong here. Quit filling my boss's ears with baloney."

"Who says it's baloney?" Buck sensed his brothers closing in—they always had each other's back. Then he caught sight of a redhead moving through the crowd. *"Destiny!"* Their gazes clashed, and he sent a silent message for her to wait for him, but she turned and walked off.

"I put my frickin' life on hold so I could convince this town to sell to Wyndell Resorts. I was this close—" Mitchell pinched his fingers together in front of Buck's nose "—to getting them to accept Custer's offer. Then you show up and get all cozy with—"

"Watch how you talk about Destiny and the others," Buck said.

"Oh, so now all these crazy idiots are your friends?" Mitchell sneered. "Or maybe you want them to think you're their friend, so they'll go along with your plans?"

"Now would be a good time to shut up," Buck said.

Mitchell curled his hands into fists and stood his ground.

"What's Mark talking about, Buck? What plans?"

Shocked that Destiny had sneaked up on him, Buck was speechless. The distrust in her eyes cut him like a knife. Didn't she know he'd never do anything to hurt her? "I put the bug in Custer's ear to consider keeping Lizard Gulch exactly where it is and incorporate the town into his plans for a resort." He winced at her quiet gasp.

"We don't want to be *owned* by Wyndell Resorts." Destiny's chin jutted.

"I don't think you will be," Buck said, having no idea what Custer's terms would be if he agreed to keep the town as is. "I suggested the town be promoted as part of the overall experience of staying at the resort."

Before Destiny had a chance to respond, Hank entered the discussion. "Buck might be onto something. I could make a lot more money if I had more customers eating at Lucille's." He nodded to Frank and Enrick who stood nearby. "The same goes for the pastry shop."

"The motel pool has a big slide. I could open it up to the kids staying at the resort and charge them a dollar to swim," Melba said, joining the conversation.

"And I could give more ghost tours," Bernie said.

"We could—"

"Shut up, all of you!" Mitchell's face burned red with anger. "I've put over a year of my life into making sure this town goes under." He spat at Buck's boots. "If you think you're going to waltz in here and push me aside, you're dumber than your namesake."

Shit. Those were fighting words.

Mitchell sucked down the rest of his beer, then spoke to the eldest Cash brother. "Heard your name is Johnny Cash." More chuckling. "How come you aren't dressed in black?"

The music stopped and silence reverberated through the air. "You're treading on thin ice, Mitchell," Buck warned.

"You!" Mitchell swung his pointer finger toward the stage.

"You got something to say to me, big shot?" Mack spoke into the microphone.

"Yes, I do, *Merle Haggard Cash.* Why would your mother name you after a no-good lawbreaking loser?"

"Excuse me, folks," Mack said. "The band's taking a short break." He set his guitar on the stage and joined his brothers.

"Don't think I haven't checked the Cashes out," Mitchell said. "Your mother was nothing but a whore, sleeping with every Tom, Dick and Harry in Arizona. Hell, you don't even know who your father is, do you, Buck Owens?"

Buck had never been close to his mother, and he didn't condone her lifestyle or understand why she'd burden her sons with the names of country-and-western legends, but a son always defended his mother's name—whether she deserved it or not.

"You get one final chance to shut up, Mitchell," Conway said.

"And if you don't," Will spoke, "we'll shut your mouth for you."

Mitchell had drunk too much or else he would have known the brothers were serious. But his ego had gotten the best of him and he spouted more garbage. "Well if it ain't Buck Owens's Buckaroos coming to his rescue."

"You were warned," Porter said. He looked at Buck. "You want to throw the first punch?"

"Can't poor little Bucky handle his own fights?" Mitchell taunted.

"As a matter of fact, he can." Buck caught Destiny's wide-eyed stare. He hated to start a fight in front of her, but his pride wouldn't allow Mitchell to walk away after the insults he'd slung. *Sorry, Destiny.* He cocked his arm and let his fist fly. His knuckles connected with Mitchell's jaw, snapping the man's head back. His beer bottle fell to the ground, and he stumbled backward into Bernie's arms. The sheriff pushed him toward Buck, and the Cash brothers circled the wagons ready to intervene if Buck needed help.

"Someone call the police!" Jim Docker showed up in the crowd. "You can't just beat up people."

"Mitchell's a crook, and so are you, Docker," Bernie said.

The Philadelphia lawyer punched the air with his fist. "You're a…a…fake sheriff!"

Bernie struck Docker in the stomach, and the man's wife screamed. A brawl broke out and Buck pinned Mitchell to the ground. The suit-and-tie guy probably hadn't visited a gym in ten years and was no match for Buck's strength.

To their credit, Buck's brothers attempted to break up the arguments and fistfights between those wanting to sell Lizard Gulch and those wanting to save the town. Several of the rodeo cowboys who'd stayed for the concert helped make sure the old people didn't get hurt.

"See what you did, Mitchell," Buck said.

"This is your fault, Cash. I don't know what's in it for you, but you'd better watch your back. No one messes with me and gets away with it."

"You gonna behave if I let you go?" Buck asked.

"Yes," Mitchell spat.

Buck stood and held out a hand to Mitchell to show there were no hard feelings, but the man spat at the gesture and got to his feet on his own.

"You mark my words, Cash. You'll regret this day." Jim and Delores Docker hurried through the parking lot with Mitchell. The three troublemakers hopped into their cars and drove off. Mack and the band struck up a lively tune, the buckle bunnies strutted their stuff and the geezers quit arguing and watched the pretty girls.

A tap on his shoulder caught Buck's attention. Destiny held out his hat to him.

"I can explain," he said.

"Maybe, but I'm not ready to listen," she said.

"When do you think you might be ready?" Buck wished his brothers weren't witnessing his dressing-down from Destiny.

"I don't know, but not tonight." She marched off.

Porter whistled. "You're in the doghouse."

"Yep," Conway said. "Looks like our brother will be sleeping under the stars later."

Buck walked off to the beer tent, his brothers' laughter ringing in his ears.

"C'MON, DESTINY. OPEN UP."

Destiny stood inside the apartment listening to Buck's pounding. For the past half hour he'd camped out on the fire escape, pleading his case. She would have thought he'd have lost his voice by now, but it was as strong and sexy as ever.

How could he have gone behind her back to negotiate a deal with Custer and not tell her? This was *her* town—not his. Buck's betrayal cut deep, especially after they'd slept together. She may have already decided that she and Buck couldn't be together because of the baby, but that hadn't prevented her from falling a little in love with him—only a little, because she wouldn't allow herself to fall all the way in love with a man she could never have.

She opened the door. "Go away, Buck." Even as she said the words she didn't have the heart to enforce them.

"I can explain. And it's not what you think."

The sooner he had his say, the sooner...what? She could tell him to leave town. Is that what she wanted? She stepped back and he entered the apartment. The poor guy looked miserable. And hot. "Do want a drink?"

"Water would be great, thanks."

Destiny grabbed a bottled water from the fridge then waited for Buck to sit on the sofa. She took the chair. Neither spoke. She was content to stare at his handsome face and memorize the shape of his lips...the tiny wrinkles fanning from the corners of his eyes...his strong cheekbones.

She admitted she'd overreacted when she accused Buck of going behind her back to negotiate a deal with Custer on behalf of the town, but she'd been desperately looking for a reason to tell Buck to leave, because each day...hour...minute she was with him, he claimed another piece of her heart.

She'd woken this morning to the gleam in his eyes and the excitement in his voice as he'd talked about the rodeo and concert, and it had hit her like a ton of bricks—Buck was a good guy. And girls like Destiny never won the good guy. They always got saddled with losers like Daryl. She'd decided right then in Buck's arms that if she couldn't have him, she didn't want any man.

She'd rather go it alone with the baby. At least she'd have her memories of Buck.

He guzzled the rest of his water then crumpled the

plastic bottle between his hands. For a man who was dying to talk, he sure was quiet. "How come you didn't tell me you'd spoken with Custer and invited him to the rodeo today?"

"I didn't want you to get your hopes up in case he hated my idea."

"And you assumed I'd go along with incorporating Lizard Gulch into the Wyndell resort plans?"

"What's the matter? You don't think it's a good idea?"

"You're a guest here—I'm the mayor. You don't have a say in the town's future, Buck. And even if you did, I had a right to know you were communicating with Custer."

"I agree." He shoved a hand through his hair. "I'm sorry."

"You made me look like a fool."

"I didn't mean to." He leaned forward on the cushion, his gaze beseeching. "You care about everyone, and you've worked so hard to save Lizard Gulch. I wanted to be the one to save the day for you."

She picked at a rip in the fabric of the chair. "I don't get why you care about—"

Buck sprang from the couch and dropped to his knees in front of her chair. "I care." He grasped her hands but didn't speak until she made eye contact. It would be so easy to lose herself in his soulful brown gaze.

"Destiny, I'm falling in love with you and this crazy town."

A lump formed in her throat. No man had ever said those words to her. In fact, no one had ever told her that they loved her. Not her mother, not Daryl, not even the

Carters when they'd adopted her. Destiny had always believed the words *I love you* were silly—until now.

"Say it again," she whispered. She'd heard him the first time, but she desperately wanted him to repeat the vow.

His vow feathered across her lips. "I'm falling in love with you."

She closed her eyes, soaking in the feel of Buck's mouth against hers. She loved his kisses, but this one was special—this one came after his declaration of love and she wanted it to last forever. He clasped her face between his hands and tilted her head. The caress grew hotter...their breathing more labored. Finally, he released her.

"You're the perfect woman for me."

Her heart sighed.

"You're gutsy, stubborn, a fearless defender of underdogs—" he tucked a strand of hair behind her ear "—and you can change a tire faster than anyone I know, including myself."

Tears burned in her eyes. "You forgot *pretty,*" she teased.

"Not pretty...striking...stunning...and that's only on the outside." He placed his fingers against her breast. "Inside, you're the most beautiful person I've ever met."

A tear leaked from her eye, but she was too caught up in Buck's gaze to care if he saw her cry.

"I've watched you treat the old people as if they're your family." Using the pad of his thumb he smeared a tear across her cheek. "I wanted to find a way to save Lizard Gulch, because it's part of you. A part that I love very much."

Was it possible for the human heart to physically

break? No one had ever given a crap about what was important to her—but Buck did, and she gathered his words close, cherishing them like a warm hug.

"I want to be a part of your life, Destiny. You've got your hands full taking care of everyone else. Let me take of you."

"Your home is in Stagecoach." After meeting his siblings and their families she didn't believe Buck would be happy living away from them for very long. "What if you get lonely for your brothers and sister?" He'd ask her to move to Stagecoach, and Destiny would be forced to pick between Lizard Gulch and him.

"My home is wherever you are." Buck thrust his fingers through Destiny's hair and pulled her mouth to his. He was losing her—he felt it with each beat of his heart. He nuzzled her lips, relieved when she relaxed her mouth and allowed him to deepen their embrace. Destiny was his soul mate, damn it, and he'd do anything to convince her that his feelings for her were the forever kind.

He used his tongue and lips to stoke the building heat between them—heat that was the result of more than chemistry. He felt a sense of desperation in her touch, and there wasn't a damn thing he could do to calm her fears.

Feeling as if he were fighting an invisible demon, he ended the kiss and stood. "I don't know any other way to show you how good we are together but to make love to you." He swooped her into his arms and carried her to the bedroom then placed her on the mattress. She looked more beautiful than ever with her red hair spread across the pillow and her big blue eyes glowing with warmth.

This time, no matter how badly his body ached for her, he wasn't rushing their lovemaking. He stood next to the bed, ready to disrobe, but Destiny got to her knees in front of him and loosened the buttons on his dress shirt then shoved the cotton material off his shoulders. She ran her hands over his chest, her short nails scratching his skin, leaving thin red lines in their wake. She leaned forward and pressed a kiss to his chest. He shivered.

She fumbled with his belt buckle, and he waited patiently for her to unclasp it. When she succeeded, he trapped her fingers against the jean zipper and waited for her to make eye contact. He needed to hear her say the words…needed to know she felt the same way about him that he felt about her. He understood that she might need more time to come to terms with her feelings, but he was certain that if he could look into her eyes and see her love for him, the words wouldn't matter.

She lifted her head and he swore the emotion swirling in her shimmering gaze was love, but there was something else…. Fear?

He cupped her face between his hands. "Don't be afraid. We're meant to be together." He sealed the pledge with a kiss then lost himself in Destiny's embrace.

DESTINY STOOD IN front of the bedroom window, watching Buck's reflection in the glass. He looked peaceful sprawled on her bed, and the image caused a searing pain in her side. For an instant she feared for the baby, but the hurt was too high in her chest—too close to her heart.

Damn it. This should never have happened. Buck had been a temporary fling. A few weeks of cowboy fun. A diversion from the stress of fighting to save the town. How had the situation spun so far out of control in such a short time? And how in the world had Buck fallen in love with *her?*

He deserved better than a girl who would lie to steal a little happiness for herself without giving a thought to the consequences. He shifted on the mattress, the sheet catching on his hips. With the taste of his kiss lingering on her lips, she approached the bed. Careful not to wake him, she caressed his bare shoulder, the length of his arm and then gently grasped his fingers. The ache in her chest expanded, eating her from the inside out. She closed her eyes and imagined Buck holding her baby, the three of them a happy family. As much as she wanted that dream, she refused to burden Buck with a child he hadn't fathered.

"Destiny! You in there? We gotta talk!"

Daryl? What was he doing here at… She turned her head toward the nightstand and squinted at the clock. Three in the morning? This couldn't be good.

She padded across the room to her closet and flung on her bathrobe then fled the room, closing the door only partway because of the squeak. "Get lost, Daryl!" she whispered after she opened the door. He swayed on the stoop. "You're drunk."

"No kidding." He hiccuped.

"I thought you'd left for California," she said.

"I did, but my mom—"

"You spoke to your mother?" As long as she'd known Daryl—granted it hadn't been long—he'd never picked up the phone and called his mom.

"I told her about the baby."

Destiny wasn't opposed to Daryl's mother learning about their child, but the timing of tonight's visit couldn't be worse.

"She wants me to do right by you."

Who was Daryl kidding? He'd never comply with his mother's wishes and marry her.

He peered behind Destiny. "Tell her, Buck."

Destiny swallowed a gasp.

"Tell Destiny what?" Buck's sleepy voice smacked her in the back of the head, and she bit her lip to keep from crying. She hadn't wanted Buck to find out about the baby.

"Tell Destiny that she has to marry me."

"You stood her up at the chapel," Buck said.

"I know." *Hiccup.* "But I gotta do right by the baby."

"What baby?" Buck's voice dropped to a whisper.

It took all of Destiny's strength to face Buck. "I'm carrying Daryl's child."

The color drained from Buck's face. His mouth parted but no words came out, then he spun and went back into the bedroom and slammed the door.

"I gotta go to California, Destiny."

"I know, Daryl."

"We should get married tomorrow."

"We'll talk about it in the morning." There was no way she'd marry Daryl no matter how good his intentions were. "Go sleep off your drunk in the cemetery."

He belched. "I don't think I can drive."

Destiny held out her hand. "Give me your car keys." He surrendered them and she watched him descend the steps.

When he reached the ground, he said, "I don't love you, Destiny."

I know, Daryl. Once he'd disappeared into the dark,

she retreated to the bedroom. Buck was sitting on the bed, dressed, staring at his boots. His shoulders were hunched as if bracing for more hurt. She wished with all her heart that time would stop and she could make sweet love with him again. She hadn't wanted his last memory of her to be tainted with anger.

She was the first to break the silence. "Buck…"

His gaze connected with hers, and the pain in his eyes stabbed her in the heart. She'd been a fool to believe she could pretend with Buck then walk away without either of them getting hurt.

"I can explain," she said, knowing she really couldn't—not in a way Buck would understand. "Daryl and I got drunk one night and ended up in his bed. It was the only time we slept together."

"If it was a one-night stand, why were you going to marry him?"

"I wanted my baby to have a father." Surely Buck wouldn't fault her for feeling that way after they'd both grown up without fathers.

He pinched the bridge of his nose and stared at the floor. "Why didn't you tell me you were pregnant?"

"I didn't expect things to go this far between us."

"And when they did?" His piercing brown gaze collided with hers. "Why didn't you say something then?"

Buck was one of the good guys. He had a generous, caring heart and deep down she'd worried that if he'd known about the baby he might offer to marry her. And Buck deserved a special woman to have a family with. Destiny wasn't special—far from it.

She shook her head until the room spun before her eyes. "I didn't tell you about the baby, because I never expected…"

"Me to fall in love with you."

Or me to fall in love with you.

"Where do we go from here?" he asked.

Most men would have stormed out of her apartment by now. Buck was giving her a chance to fix what she'd done. If she confessed that she'd fallen in love with him he'd stay in Lizard Gulch with her. He'd forgive her for everything.

Exasperated, she spoke without thinking. "Buck, this was never supposed to be anything but a good time."

He gawked at her.

She knew every word out of her mouth was a bullet straight into Buck's heart. She had to end this before she begged him to stay. "I'm going to marry Daryl." She swallowed the bile that rose in her throat from the lie.

"But you said you didn't love him."

"He's the father of my baby."

"So it doesn't matter that I love you, and Daryl doesn't?"

Why was he making this so hard?

He went to the closet and reached inside for his duffel bag, filled with clothes she'd recently washed for him, then he left the bedroom and walked through the living room. He paused at the door, his hand on the knob as if he hoped she'd stop him.

Dear God, just go, Buck. Please.

Then he was gone.

The tears pressing against Destiny's eyes finally broke free and dribbled down her cheeks.

Chapter Thirteen

"Well, look who the haboob blew in," Mack said when Buck entered the bunkhouse Sunday night.

"Things are getting pretty bad if you and Porter are the only ones playing poker." Buck had left Lizard Gulch the morning after the rodeo and had driven aimlessly across the state, hoping he'd forget Destiny. After seven hundred miles he'd raised the white flag and had headed home to Stagecoach. It wasn't until his truck whizzed past Vern's Drive-In that he admitted Southern Arizona no longer felt like home.

"Did Destiny come with you?" Porter asked.

"No." Buck set the duffel bag by his bed and stared at the rodeo posters he'd helped select to decorate the bachelor pad. He'd had a lot of good times in the bunkhouse, but the familiar sense of comfort was missing.

"Don't keep us in suspense," Mack said. "What happened with Lizard Gulch? Did the townspeople vote to sell to the developer or not?"

"I don't know." Buck helped himself to a beer.

"What do you mean, you don't know?" Porter said. "Aren't you tight with the mayor?"

Buck slammed the fridge door and ignored his brothers' frowns.

"Did you two have a fight?" Mack asked.

Buck expected a grilling about his extended absence from the farm, but he wasn't in the mood to discuss his relationship with Destiny. He sat on his bed, back propped against the wall and stared into space.

"They had a fight," Porter whispered to Mack then said, "for what it's worth, I liked Destiny. She's a cool chick."

"Porter, when are you going to grow up?" Buck asked.

"What do mean?"

"Cool chick?" Buck mimicked his brother's voice. "You talk like a teenager."

"Did she cheat on you?" Porter asked.

Buck flew off the bed, tackled his brother and they rolled across the rug on the floor.

"Knock it off, guys." Mack put a stop to the brawl. "What's gotten into you, Buck? You never pick fights."

The bunkhouse door opened, and Conway waltzed in, wearing a huge grin.

"What are you so happy about?" Buck asked.

"Isi's pregnant."

Porter crawled to his feet. "Is she having twins?"

"Yep."

"For a man who swore he'd never have kids, you're gonna be father to a whole passel of rugrats." Mack slapped Conway on the back then the brothers bumped fists. "Girls or boys?"

"Don't know yet."

Buck slunk off to a corner and tried to block out the conversation.

"How far along is she?" Porter asked.

"Three and a half months. Isi didn't want to tell me

until she knew for sure everything was okay with the pregnancy."

"Whoo-hoo!" Porter danced a jig. "I'm gonna be an uncle again."

"You wait, baby brother," Conway said. "Your turn at fatherhood is coming."

"The next brother who ties the knot will be Mack or Buck," Porter said. "Not me."

"It's gonna happen sooner or later to all of you," Conway said. "You'll fall in love with a woman, and your whole world will turn upside down."

Buck's world had already been turned upside down, and he'd been dumped on his head. Right now he wished he was anywhere but in the bunkhouse.

Mack nudged Buck's arm. "Aren't you going to congratulate Conway?"

"Congratulations." Buck's voice was devoid of excitement.

"Did Destiny come home with you?" Conway asked.

"No." Porter and Mack answered for Buck.

"I don't want to talk about it," Buck said.

"Maybe you should speak to Will. He feels bad that he made you leave town," Conway said.

"Where are Will and Marsha living?" Buck asked.

"They're renting a house in Stagecoach," Conway said.

There were only two streets with homes in town. "Which house?"

Porter chuckled. "The one next to Fiona Wilson."

The retired English teacher was dating Shannon's father. "Guess I'll head into town and pay Will a visit." Anything was better than hanging around his happy brothers.

Mack stepped in front of Buck, blocking his path. "We're here if you need to talk."

His brothers meant well, and Buck felt bad for being an ass. "Thanks." He made eye contact with Conway. "I'm happy for you and Isi."

"We're grilling out tonight. You gonna eat with us?"

He shook his head. "I don't have much of an appetite." Buck left the bunkhouse and made a beeline for his truck before his brothers found an excuse to keep him at the farm. He wasn't used to seeking advice, but he felt like a ticking time bomb that might explode at any minute. Maybe Will could help him screw his head back on straight.

Fifteen minutes later Buck pulled up to his brother's house and studied the ranch-style home. The stucco structure wasn't fancy, but it appeared well kept. There was no garage—just a carport and Will's truck sat beneath the cover. Buck parked on the street. He didn't notice Fiona Wilson kneeling in her flower bed until he was halfway across Will's yard.

"Is that you, Buck Owens?"

"Hello, Ms. Wilson."

The older woman smiled and waved her pruning shears. She wore a big floppy hat that hid half her face from view and a pair of pink gardening gloves.

"Will got home a few minutes ago. Ryan and Marsha are at the pastor's house."

His brother must love having a neighbor who kept tabs on him and his family's whereabouts. "Thanks." Buck continued across the yard toward the porch steps.

"I heard you moved to a small town near Kingman," Fiona said.

"I didn't move there, ma'am. I was visiting a friend."

Fiona frowned. "Oh. I thought you were sweet on a girl up there." She got to her feet. "I ran into Marsha at the hair salon, and she said the whole family had a wonderful time at the rodeo in…" Fiona shook her head. "I can't recall the name of the town—"

"Lizard Gulch." If he didn't help the conversation along, he'd be stuck talking to the woman for an hour.

"That's right. Lizard Gulch. Strange name for a town." She swatted at a bug near her face. "Anyway, Marsha said the town was in some kind of trouble and you were trying to save it from being bought by a developer."

Gotta love the Stagecoach gossip mill. By the end of the day Buck's disastrous love life would be the new hot topic. Not wanting to add to the rumors, he took the easy way out. "The town's taking care of itself, Ms. Wilson."

"How old are you again?"

"Thirty-one, ma'am."

"I believe you're old enough to call me by my first name."

Where the hell was his brother? Buck punched the doorbell. "Yes, ma'am. I mean, Fiona."

"Have you been out to the Triple D to see little Addy?" Buck didn't have a chance to answer before she continued her spiel, "That baby is such a sweetheart, and she's got her granddaddy wrapped around her finger."

C'mon, Will. Hurry up and open the door.

"Why you should see all the little frilly dresses Clive's bought for Addy, and she won't be big enough to wear them for another year or two." Fiona wiped her brow. "Between you and me, I think Clive's trying his best to make sure Addy doesn't turn into a tomboy like her mother."

"You don't say," Buck mumbled.

"Just the other day Clive caught Johnny putting Addy on the mechanical bull, and I thought Clive was going to have a heart attack. Johnny insists it calms Addy down when she's in the middle of one of her colicky fits, but—"

"You're back," Will said, after he opened the door. *Thank God.*

Will spoke to his neighbor. "How's the garden coming along, Fiona?"

"Fine, Will. My rosebushes have bloomed four times this summer."

"That's great," Will said.

"You boys have a nice visit." Fiona knelt in the flower bed and continued pruning the bushes.

Buck stepped inside his brother's house, and as soon as the door closed, he said, "You've got to be nuts living next to that woman."

"She's not so bad. You want a drink?"

He'd like another beer, but he hadn't finished the one he'd opened in the bunkhouse. "No." When they reached the galley kitchen, Buck said, "This is a decent place."

"There's plenty of room for the three of us."

"You don't act surprised to see me."

"Porter texted that you were on your way." Will opened the back door and stepped onto a screened-in porch.

"Hey, this is nice." Buck sat on the couch and Will took the chair.

"So you broke up with Destiny?"

"Hard to break up with someone when you weren't even dating," Buck said.

"I thought you two were a couple."

"Turns out I was a nothing but a fling."

Will's eyebrows rose.

Buck popped off the couch and paced across the porch. How did he explain something he didn't even understand? Twice he opened his mouth to speak but the words wouldn't come out.

"What the hell, Buck. Just say it."

"Destiny's pregnant."

"That was fast work on your part."

"The baby's not mine. It's Daryl's."

"Who's Daryl?"

"The stupid ass who left Destiny at the altar the afternoon she rescued me from the side of the road."

Will grinned.

"You think this is funny?"

"No." His brother schooled his expression. "But you have to admit, it's a little comical…a girl coming to your rescue."

"Be serious, Will."

"Fine. Did this Daryl guy change his mind about marrying Destiny?"

Buck gaped. "How'd you know?"

"You said he'd left her at the altar." Will shrugged. "Which means Destiny must have taken this Daryl guy back if he changed his mind about marriage."

"She doesn't love him, Will. She just wants her baby to have a father."

"Does Destiny love you?"

Buck rubbed his brow. "She never came right out

and said the words." He pounded his chest with his fist. "But I know she does. I felt it when we—"

"Whoa, brother. No need for specifics. I get what you're saying."

Buck stared through the screen into the backyard. He couldn't have been wrong about Destiny loving him— it had been there in her eyes when she'd watched him walk out her door.

"What did she say when you told her that you loved her?" Will asked.

"She said what we shared was never meant to be anything more than a good time."

"Ouch."

Ouch didn't come close to describing the pain Destiny's confession had inflicted. *But those were just words—words meant to drive you away.* If only he could be sure.

"What are you going to do?"

Buck laughed because if he didn't, he'd break down and embarrass himself. "That's why I'm here. You're supposed to tell me what to do."

"Hey, I screwed things up so badly with Marsha, it's a miracle she's giving me a second chance."

"I just want a first chance with Destiny." He shoved his fingers through his hair. "You should see Daryl. The guy's got rocks for a brain."

Chuckling, Will asked, "Are you afraid the baby will take after his father?"

"The kid's going to need a strong, steady hand to make sure he turns out right." Buck stared at his brother. There was no need to explain what he was feeling—he and his brothers had all dealt with this demon.

"You don't believe Daryl's good enough to be the

kid's father, but you're not sure you are, either." When Buck remained silent, Will said, "Look at Conway. The boys love him like he was their real birth father. You could have the same thing with Destiny and her baby if you don't let your fears get the best of you."

"I told Destiny that it didn't bother me that I've gone through life not knowing who my father is," Buck said.

"But it does bother you."

"Yeah."

"So when Destiny confessed that she was marrying Daryl because of the baby, you latched on to that as an excuse to let her push you away?"

Buck didn't want to admit his brother might be right. "She picked Daryl, not me."

"Do you want to be with Destiny? Is she the one you envision spending the rest of your life with?"

"I thought so."

"You can't think so, Buck, you have to know so. If she's the one, then you fight your fears and convince her that's she's picked the wrong guy."

Marsha's voice echoed through the house before Buck could respond. "We're back, Will!" She stepped onto the porch and her eyes lit up. "Buck, you're home."

He forced a smile, even though his gut had twisted into a giant pretzel. The word *home* didn't have the same feeling as it had before he'd hit the road earlier in the summer. "Marsha." He gave her a brotherly hug. "Welcome to the Cash clan."

"You want me to call you Uncle Buck?" Ryan laughed.

Buck stared at Will. "Did he see the movie?"

"Dad rented *Uncle Buck* for me a few weeks ago."

"Thanks, Will. Thanks a whole bunch." Buck ruffled Ryan's hair. "I think just plain Buck will do."

"I made a casserole for supper," Marsha said. "We'd love for you to eat with us."

"I don't want to interrupt—"

"You should stay, *Uncle* Buck." Ryan snickered. "I want to show you the rocket my dad and I built this summer. The model's three feet long."

It warmed Buck's heart to hear Ryan call Will *Dad*. Marsha, Will and Ryan had become the family they were always meant to be. "Sure, kid."

As Buck walked out of the room, he heard Marsha say, "Is everything okay between you two?"

"Yep," Will said. "The family's all good, honey."

Family. The word reverberated inside Buck's head as he entered his nephew's room. Buck had family—siblings who would be there for him through good and bad. Destiny had no one—just her and the baby. No matter what Daryl said or promised, the deadbeat dad would take off the first chance he got. A picture of Destiny holding a small child in her arms flashed before Buck's eyes.

The lonely image left him feeling scared and a little desperate.

"Quiet! Please be quiet!" Destiny stood at the bar inside Lucille's and waited for the group to settle down. "I organized this meeting at the request of Jack Custer." The developer had arrived in town less than an hour ago.

"What happened to Mitchell and the Dockers?" Bernie called out.

Custer stepped in front of Destiny. "Mark no longer

works for Wyndell Resorts. From now on, you people are dealing directly with me."

"Let Destiny talk," Melba said. "She's our mayor and we listen to her, not you."

Before things became ugly, Destiny said, "Calm down. We've got a big decision to make today, and we're going to need everyone thinking clearly." The saloon grew quiet. "As you all know, the rodeo and concert were a huge success two weekends ago and—"

"Where's Buck, Destiny?" Sonja asked.

"Yeah, Buck should be here. The fund-raiser was his idea," Bernie said. "He's earned a vote in what happens to the town."

Destiny had fielded questions all week regarding Buck's whereabouts, and she was tired of pretending that they had just been friends. "Buck won't be back." She grimaced at the sea of blank stares.

"Did you two have a fight?" Enrick asked.

Hank moved from behind the bar. "If Buck stepped over the line with you…say the word and I'll find him."

Tears burned Destiny's eyes. She loved that her friends were concerned about her, but she was also aware of how much they'd enjoy having Buck in town. If they knew the real reason he'd left—because she'd lied about marrying Daryl and had told him to go— they'd be upset with her. It was bad enough that she'd lost Buck. She didn't want to lose her new family, too.

"Can we stop talking about Destiny and her love life, for God's sake," Custer grumbled.

Destiny cleared her throat. "As you know, we raised enough money to hire a lawyer to represent Lizard Gulch and file a lawsuit against Wyndell Resorts in hopes of preventing Mr. Custer from bulldozing the town."

Everyone talked at once, then Hank slammed an empty beer pitcher against the bar and thunderous silence rippled through the room. "When Mr. Custer discovered we'd hired a lawyer," Destiny said, "he decided to change his plans for the resort."

"I bet the pansy did!" Melba snarled.

"Please allow Mr. Custer a chance to explain his ideas for the resort. Then we'll vote on the future of Lizard Gulch."

Custer straightened his shoulders. "I'm willing to build my resort around the town and leave—" he spread his arms wide "—all the buildings and trailers right where they are, with the understanding that resort guests be allowed access to the town if they should choose to come over here and visit." He paused as if expecting applause or cheers rather than the silence that greeted his announcement. "No one will have to leave their home, unless they want to."

"You gonna make everyone tidy up their places?" Melba asked.

"No." Destiny sent Custer a warning look. "Not unless you want to. If your home needs repairs, but you don't have the money, Mr. Custer has graciously agreed to set up a Lizard Gulch beautification fund, which the town council can use at their discretion."

Hank raised his hand. "Does the money include repairs to our businesses?"

"Yes," Destiny said.

"If I'm going to be serving more customers, I'll need a new fryer and a deep freeze." Hank spoke to Custer.

"The bar, the bakery and the motel have the green

light to update their properties to accommodate more customers," Custer said.

"What about the cemetery?" Bernie asked. "Don't I get some money to make improvements, too?"

"What the hell kind of improvements do you need to make to three grave markers and a tree?" Custer asked.

Destiny caught Melba and Bernie exchanging a conspiratorial look. She suspected any improvements made to the graveyard would benefit the ghost tour and enhance the ghostly tale of Maisy and her lovers' showdown at the motel.

"We could use a stone bench for people to sit on when they visit the graves," Bernie said.

Custer shook his head in disgust. "Fine. You want a bench? I'll give you a bench."

"What about one of them fancy mister systems for my trailer?"

"Bernie, get serious," Destiny said. "It's time for a vote. All those in favor of allowing Wyndell Resorts to build in our backyard, raise your hand."

Hank was the first to lift his arm, then Enrick, Frank, Bernie and Melba. After a tense few seconds, the rest of the town joined in a unanimous vote.

"Looks like you have your decision." Destiny shook Custer's hand. "But before you move forward with your plans, I'll need your lawyer to contact our lawyer. I'm making sure you keep your promises."

"This will be a win-win deal for everyone." Custer spun on his heels and left the saloon.

The fact that Lizard Gulch would continue to exist was Buck's doing, and Destiny would always be grateful he'd cared enough to help the friends who'd become her adopted family. A family with one member missing—Buck.

"You've been this town's good-luck charm since you settled here, Destiny," Bernie said.

Good luck? Hardly.

"You saved Lizard Gulch." Melba turned to the group. "Three cheers for Destiny!"

When the raucous noise died down, Destiny said, "You're wrong. Buck saved this town." Before she fell apart, she fled through the back door of the bar. No sooner had she entered her apartment above the garage than a knock sounded at the door. Melba had followed her home.

"C'mon in."

As soon as Melba stepped inside, her gaze searched the space.

"Don't worry. Buck's not hiding here. He left for good."

"I saw him drive off a few days ago, but I assumed he was heading to a rodeo and that he'd be back."

I wish.

"What happened? You were getting along like two peas in a pod, tinkering with cars and playing miniature golf."

Memories of lying next to Buck on their creepers beneath Bernie's car brought tears to Destiny's eyes. Good grief—everything made her cry these days. *Blasted pregnancy hormones.*

Melba sat on the couch and patted the cushion next to her. "What happened?"

Destiny had held everything inside for too long and she felt as if she'd burst if she didn't vent. "I'm pregnant."

Melba gasped. "Hank will go after Buck and make him do right by you or—"

"The baby isn't Buck's, Melba. It's Daryl's."

"But Daryl stood you up at the altar!"

"Then he came back and said he'd marry me, because his mother had told him to."

Melba gasped. "Don't tell me you agreed to tie the knot with him."

"I have no intention of marrying Daryl, but I lied to Buck and said I was going to."

"Did Buck know you were carrying Daryl's baby?"

"Not until the day he left."

Melba gasped. "The whole time you and Buck were together, he didn't know you were pregnant?"

"I didn't think it was important, because he was only staying in town a few weeks—until his truck was repaired." *And I never expected to fall in love with him.*

"But why did you lie to Buck about marrying Daryl?"

"Because…" The truth hurt.

Melba narrowed her eyes. "Do you love Buck?"

"Yes."

"Does he love you?"

"He said he did."

"Well, this is ridiculous." Melba rolled her eyes. "Then tell me the real reason you sent him away."

Destiny wiped her eyes. "Look at me, Melba. I'm not good enough for Buck. He deserves better than a girl who's lived in truck stops—"

"You lived in a truck stop?"

"My mother was a prostitute. I have no idea which one of her customers is my father."

"As far as childhoods go, yours certainly stunk, but what does how you were raised have to do with believing you aren't good enough for Buck?" Melba sprang from her seat. "The Destiny I'm looking at right now is strong, loyal and caring." She patted her chest. "Young lady, your heart is bigger than the state of Arizona."

Destiny's throat tightened. No one had ever said anything so nice to her before.

"You're a fool if you allow Buck to get away." Melba marched across the room and let herself out the door.

Destiny stared into space. She'd gone it alone for so long, she didn't know how to trust that Buck's love for her was real. She admitted that she'd taken the coward's way out—it had been much easier to push him away than to live with the fear of him one day leaving her.

Melba was right—she'd be a fool to let Buck slip away. Worse…could she live with herself if she didn't give her and Buck a chance at their very own happy ever after?

Chapter Fourteen

Three weeks had passed since Buck had left Lizard Gulch, and Destiny had been front and center of his every thought every minute of every day.

> Wyndell Properties announces the construction of its newest resort, Apache Springs, located next to the town of Lizard Gulch, Arizona—a Route 66 landmark.

Buck sat on the edge of his bed and stared at the postcard Melba had sent him. He was relieved to learn that Custer and Destiny had negotiated a deal and Lizard Gulch would be spared the wrecking ball. The eccentric folks who'd retired in the small town wouldn't have to relocate and could remain one big happy family—Destiny's family.

Buck hated the way things had ended with Destiny, but at least now when he thought of her, he could envision her living above the garage and eating at Lucille's. Or talking with Melba outside the motel office. Driving her wrecker and towing cars along the same highway he'd gotten stranded. And he was relieved she'd have help raising her baby—he doubted Daryl the loser would stick around long after he and Destiny tied the knot.

As for who would take care of him? As much as he loved his siblings, their concern smothered him. Each time one of his brothers sent him a sympathetic look, he felt like punching a brick wall.

Maybe Buck hadn't left the farm to find the woman of his dreams, but he'd met Destiny and damn it, she was *the one.* So Destiny had only meant to flirt with him in the beginning, believing he'd go on his way before he found out she was pregnant, but she'd crossed the line when she'd made love to him…when she'd allowed him to fall in love with her.

"Buck?" Conway poked his head inside the bunkhouse.

"Yeah, I'm here."

Conway's gaze landed on the rodeo gear next to the bed. "Where are you going?"

"Back on the circuit." Until he figured out his next move.

His brother stepped inside and let the screen door slam behind him. "You just came home."

"I can't stay." He had to keep moving—that was the only decent chance he had of outrunning the memories.

"You're not going to get far," Conway said.

"Why's that?"

"There's a roadblock with your name on it out in the yard."

Roadblock? Buck went to the window. "What the hell?" Half the town of Lizard Gulch stood in front of the farmhouse.

"They're demanding a word with you."

"How'd they get here?" He didn't see any vehicles other than his brothers' pickups.

"They chartered a bus. It's parked out on the road by the mailbox."

Buck retrieved his cowboy hat from the bed, then hefted his gear bag over his shoulder and left the bunkhouse. When the group spotted him, they stopped talking. He dropped the bag at his feet and faced off with the pack leader. "Melba."

She planted her hands on her hips. "We never figured you for a coward, Buck Owens Cash."

Aware he had an audience—Isi and the boys sat on the porch swing. Mack leaned against the porch rail, and Conway and Porter flanked his side.

"If this is about what happened between me and Destiny—"

"You broke that poor girl's heart." Enrick waved a hand wildly in the air. "Why that girl was so distraught, she wouldn't stop crying and—"

Frank slapped Enrick on the back. "Shut up and stop lying. He knows Destiny doesn't cry."

But her eyes had watered when she'd confirmed her pregnancy to Buck.

Hank cleared his throat. "We know about the baby."

"Then you know it's not mine," Buck said.

Melba nodded.

"So you're talking to the wrong man. Destiny told me she's marrying Daryl."

"We're not letting Destiny marry Daryl. He's got loser—" Bernie's fingers formed the letter *L* "—written all over him."

"We love Destiny." Melba stepped closer to Buck,

her eyes pleading with him. "She's one of us. And we want her to be happy."

"What am I supposed to do, Melba?"

"Convince Destiny to pick you over Daryl."

"She's not carrying my baby."

"Does it matter whose baby it is, if you love Destiny?" Melba asked.

Didn't they understand that Destiny chose Daryl—not him?

"You're the only man who's good enough for our Destiny. And you'll make sure that baby doesn't turn out like Daryl the dunce," Hank said.

"The baby will be lucky to have you for a father," Violet spoke up.

Bernie stepped forward. "You're a good man, Buck Owens. We need more men like you in Lizard Gulch."

"You're all making it sound so easy," Buck said.

"It is easy." Melba placed her hand on Buck's arm and stared him in the eye. "I know you love Destiny. And if you love that girl, then you love all of her, including Daryl's baby."

There was no doubt in Buck's mind that he loved Destiny and he didn't give a crap who fathered her baby—the child was a part of Destiny, and he'd love the baby as if it was his own. What he didn't know for sure...what scared him the most was fatherhood. He didn't know the first thing about being a father. What if he screwed up with the baby? He loved Destiny too much to risk failing her child. "I need to think about it, Melba."

"If you love Destiny but you need to think about it, then you're not half the man we thought you were." Melba faced the group. "Our business is done here."

She waved everyone toward the dirt path that led to the waiting bus.

"Melba." When she stopped and turned, Buck said, "Destiny never planned to tell me about the baby, and she knew I was falling in love with her."

"She was protecting her own heart, Buck. Everyone she's known has let her down."

"Not you." Buck pointed to the group walking away. "Not them."

"True, but she's not in love with us. She's in love with you." Melba spun, but Buck snagged her arm.

"When are they getting married?"

"I don't know. She hasn't said anything to any of us." Melba pulled her arm free and hurried after the group.

Buck faced his brothers. "Well? I know you're all dying to tell me what to do."

No one said a word or moved a muscle. Fine. He was tired of talking anyway. He put his duffel and rodeo gear in the truck.

"Where you going?" Conway asked.

"Winslow." He'd already paid the entry fee to three rodeos—one this last weekend in September and the first two weekends in October. "After Winslow I'm heading to Douglas then Colorado City."

"You'll use up more money in gas, driving to each rodeo than you will on entry fees," Mack said.

That had been his plan all along—stay in the truck and drive for hours between each rodeo, praying the miles and miles of blacktop would help him forget Destiny.

"Maybe you should stay a few more days at the farm, before you go off half-cocked," Conway said.

"I can't."

"What about Troy?" Porter asked. "Did you tell him you were leaving again?"

"I gave Troy my two weeks' notice when I got back to town."

Porter gaped. "You quit for good?"

"Yep. Troy understands."

"Good for Troy," Mack said. "Now make us understand."

"Until I know for sure what I want, I'm no good to anybody." Buck opened the driver's side door and hopped in.

"You sure in hell won't do any good on the back of a bronc, either," Mack said.

"I'll be fine."

"Are you gonna answer our calls and texts this time?" Conway asked.

"I'm not dropping off the face of the earth. I gave you my itinerary. I'll check in after each rodeo."

"You'd better." Mack reached inside the truck and squeezed Buck's shoulder. "Drive safely."

By the time Buck backed out of the yard and reached the highway, the motor coach was a speck on the horizon. He turned in the opposite direction and drove out of town. He had two days to make it to Winslow, and he was in no hurry. When the speedometer reached eighty-five, he moved his foot off the gas. No sense arriving for the rodeo early—he'd have nothing to do but stare at motel room walls and think about Destiny.

DESTINY PULLED OFF the road and stopped the Harley next to the mailbox with black magnetic letters that spelled CASH. The weirdo at the gas station in Stagecoach had told her to take the dirt road after a billboard advertising Vera's Lounge for Gentlemen. This had to be the pecan farm. She checked her side mirrors—nothing but miles of asphalt in either direction.

What if Buck doesn't want to see me? What if he tells me to leave?

After everything she'd been through in her life, being told to get lost was nothing. Brave words for a woman who was shaking in her biker boots. She loved Buck, and if he told her to get lost she'd be devastated. She didn't care that her mother didn't love her. She didn't care that Daryl didn't love her.

She cared that Buck loved her.

But that was before he knew about the baby.

And that's why she'd come to the farm. She had to find out if there was the slightest chance that Buck would forgive her for lying to him about her pregnancy. And if he did forgive her, then she'd ask him if he could love her, knowing the baby she carried wasn't his.

And if he could do both then she was going to ask him to marry her.

A truck honked then pulled off the road and stopped next to her. The passenger window lowered. "Destiny?"

The driver was Buck's brother, Will.

"Is Buck here?" she asked.

"Follow me."

She shifted gears and drove behind the pickup along a dirt road lined with pecan trees. When they entered a yard, she saw a farmhouse, barn and large metal shed. A black Lab slept on the roof of his doghouse beneath a tree near the porch.

If she were Buck, she'd never want to leave this place.

Will got out of his truck, and Destiny set the kickstand on her bike. "Buck might be in the bunkhouse," he said.

Destiny walked with him to the shed then Will opened the door and motioned her to go inside first. "Guess who dropped by the farm," he said when the door closed behind them.

The Cash brothers playing cards at the table spoke simultaneously. "Destiny."

"Porter and Mack." Will pointed out each brother. "Where's Buck?"

Mack glared at Porter. "Didn't you tell Will?"

"I thought you were gonna tell Will," Porter said.

Will waved his hand. "Tell me what?"

"Buck's not here," Porter said. "He went back to rodeo. Left yesterday."

"Do you know when he plans to return?" Destiny asked.

"Not anytime soon," Mack said.

Will stared at his brothers. "Is he still upset with what happened between us earlier in the summer?"

"His leaving had nothing to do with you, Will," Mack said.

"It's me, isn't it?" Destiny whispered.

"Buck said he needed time to think." Porter flashed a sympathetic smile.

Destiny felt like crying.

"Where's his first rodeo?" Will asked.

"Winslow," Mack said.

"You could call him, Destiny," Porter said.

"I have. He's not picking up or answering my texts." She couldn't stand seeing the pity in the brothers' eyes. She reached for the door.

"Where are you going?" Will asked.

"To find Buck."

Porter grinned. "You go, girl."

If she wasn't so scared Buck would reject her, she might have laughed at Porter's comment.

"Please don't warn Buck that I'm coming for him." She didn't want to risk him being a no-show at the rodeo in Winslow because he knew she was on her way there.

Mack grinned. "Mum's the word."

Destiny walked over to her bike and put on her helmet—a baby shower gift from Melba. Now that she was going to be a mother, Melba had insisted she take her safety into consideration when she rode the Harley. While she buckled the strap, she heard Will say, "I'd give a month's wages to see the look on Buck's face when Destiny shows up at the rodeo."

Depending on what that look was, Destiny would give her soul for it, too.

"Folks that was All-Around Cowboy C. J. Rodriguez who made it to eight on Red Devil! Looks like the judges are gonna give the cowboy an eighty-four for his effort. Eight-four puts Rodriguez in second place."

Buck ignored the announcer's voice as he rubbed resin on his riding glove. He was second-guessing his decision to enter the bull riding event—not that a rank bronc was any easier, but at least the horses didn't try to freight train their riders.

"'My Heart Skips a Beat,' it's Buck Owens Cash."

Rodriguez. The man was a cocky son of a gun with a shady past who loved to pick a fight. If he wasn't so talented in rodeo, he'd probably be in prison right now.

"Did I hear right? You wanna be a bull rider today?"

Rodriguez stepped in front of Buck, making it impossible to ignore the jerk.

"You heard right." Buck wondered if his brother Johnny had challenged Rodriguez to a ride-off, because it had been the only way to shut the man up.

"How's married life treating the Man in Black?"

Buck stared Rodriguez in the eye. "You ever get tired of mocking people?"

The bull rider grinned, then when he realized he didn't have an audience he lost the smile. "How's Shannon? Is she ready to compete again?"

Buck laughed. "I don't think she has any plans to get back into bull riding—at least not for a while."

"Is the leg she broke bothering her?"

"It's not her leg keeping her out of rodeo. She had a baby."

"No kidding. Boy or girl?"

Even though Rodriguez gave Shannon a hard time when they'd traveled the circuit together, Buck sensed the cowboy respected her—probably because she was the only person who put up with his crap. Rumors claimed that the popular-with-the-ladies rodeo star was friendless.

"Shannon had a little girl. Named her Addy after our grandmother."

"Addy. That's nice. Tell Shannon congratulations for me."

After Rodriguez walked off, Buck focused on the bull he'd drawn. Destiny's Curse—man, oh, man had he been surprised to read the name on the livestock list. Just like the bull, Destiny had put a curse on Buck, and no matter that he'd tried to forget her, he couldn't. Since leaving Lizard Gulch he'd been unsuccessful in evicting Destiny from his heart or his head. And the one place he'd believed he'd be safe from her memory—rodeo—he wasn't.

The solid black bull—not a spec of white anywhere on his body—pawed the dirt inside the chute. Maybe the bull was a sign that Buck had to face his demons. He was only using the excuse of Destiny not being truthful with him about the baby as a shield against his real fear. How could he convince Destiny to believe that they were meant to be together if he didn't believe in himself?

"Folks, one of our judges had an emergency. It'll be a minute or two before our next bull ride. Hold tight. We'll get this show on the road soon." After the announcer spoke, music blared over the sound system.

Swell. More time for the voices in his head to interfere with his concentration.

Buck edged closer to the chute. The bull swung his massive head sideways and stared Buck down with lifeless eyes. He thought of Destiny's blue eyes—eyes full of life, sparkle, humor and compassion.

A jarring pain stabbed him in the chest. He'd been labeled the family peacemaker by his siblings because he didn't like confrontation. Hell, when he'd been teased and bullied on the playground he'd tried turning the other cheek or walking away. If the bullies wouldn't let him flee, then he stood his ground and fought back. Was the instinct to run a genetic trait he'd inherited from his father and mother? Shoot, when his mother had been alive, she'd never confronted the men who'd gotten her pregnant and demanded they make an honest woman out of her. Or demand they play a role in their sons' lives. She just left them and moved on.

Buck had used the excuse of Destiny not telling him about her pregnancy to split. Even though he'd confessed his love for her, he'd been afraid to stay and fight for a place in her life, and it had nothing to do with Destiny not confessing her love for him. Buck knew in his gut that she loved him—he'd seen it in every look and touch she'd given him during his time in Lizard Gulch. Buck even suspected she had his best interests at heart when she sent him away.

It would be easy to believe Destiny didn't want to burden him with raising Daryl's baby, but Buck feared the real reason she'd kicked him out of her life was because she sensed he wouldn't always be there for her. And since she didn't love Daryl, it wouldn't be a big deal if he packed up and left her.

The music died down and the announcer spoke, "Well, folks, it looks like we've got our judge back and we're ready for the next contestant!" The crowd applauded. "It's time for Buck Cash from Stagecoach, Arizona, to cowboy up!" Boots stomped on the metal bleachers creating an earsplitting din. "Cash is ridin' Destiny's Curse, a bull known for its tight spins."

Buck closed his eyes and envisioned the ride in his head. It took three tries before his brain replaced Destiny's pretty face with the bull's big head. He felt the cameras zero in on him, but refused to look at his image on the JumboTron. As he focused, the noise in the arena dissipated until the only sound he heard was the bull's snorting.

"I can't figure out if good ol' Buck is dreaming about his bull ride or that lady gal standing behind him." The announcer's voice disrupted Buck's concentration. The crowd hooted and hollered.

Buck opened his eyes and glanced at the giant screen at the opposite end of the arena. He blinked twice, unable to believe what he was looking at. Slowly he turned and came face-to-face with Destiny.

"Never seen a cowgirl in that kind of getup before," the announcer said.

Buck's gaze soaked in the sight of her—black leather pants, a tight vest that showed a hint of cleavage, high-heeled boots and fringed leather gloves up to her elbows. Was it any wonder his competitors in the cowboy ready area stood gawking?

This is your chance. Don't blow it.

Buck forced his legs to move and he closed the distance between them. Destiny's eyes shone with tears, and he couldn't help himself from touching her—didn't care who watched him. He tucked a strand of flaming hair behind her ear. "We're not through—you and me."

"I was hoping you'd say that."

"Wait right here, while I take care of this bull, then we'll talk."

"Be careful, Buck. I don't want anything to happen to you."

"Darlin', a bull doesn't stand a chance against a man who's in love." He kissed her, careful to angle his head so his cowboy hat blocked the cameras. The fans in the arena roared their approval.

He ended the kiss, then with a burst of energy, climbed the rails and eased onto the back of the bull. "You and me are gonna get along just fine," he whispered, wrapping the rope around his gloved hand.

The gate opened, and Destiny's Curse bolted for freedom. The announcer hadn't been fooling when he'd claimed the bull was a spinner. Buck ground his teeth together and leaned back as he rode out the first spin. His hat flew off, but he held on and the bull rotated into a second spin.

Go all the way for Destiny. Show her you're not a quitter.

The bull came out of the spin, kicking his back legs at the same time he twisted his spine. Even an experienced world champion bull rider would have had trouble handling this monster, but Buck was riding on a cloud of euphoria and found the strength to hang on.

He hadn't taken a breath since the bull left the chute, and his lungs burned with the need for oxygen. He lost track of the seconds in his head and when the buzzer clanged, no one was more excited than him that he'd made it to eight. He waited for an opening, but the bull's spinning was relentless and Buck decided he'd have to take a leap of faith. He launched himself into the air and hit the ground hard, the impact releasing what little air remained in his lungs. Instinct kicked in and he rolled away from the bull, allowing the bullfighters to step in and distract Destiny's Curse. When he crawled to his knees he saw that the bull had lost interest in him and had trotted toward to the bull pen. Buck swept his hat off the ground and waved it at the crowd.

"Looks like Buck Owens Cash got the best of Destiny's Curse," the announcer said. "Let's see what the judges award him."

Buck didn't care about his score. The only thing that mattered was the woman waiting for him in the cowboy ready area. Buck scaled the arena rail and when his boots hit the ground on the other side, Destiny launched herself into his arms.

"Buck Owens Cash earned an eighty-three for his

performance on Destiny's Curse," the announcer said. "That's good enough for third place." The announcer chuckled. "But it looks like he's won first place with the girl!"

Music blared throughout the arena, and the fans cheered.

Buck hugged Destiny tighter, afraid to let her go.

"Oh, my God, Buck, please tell me you're never going to ride another bull again." She leaned back and clasped his face in her hands. "I died a hundred deaths, waiting for you to fly off and get trampled."

"Have a little faith in me, honey." Buck stared into her shimmering blue eyes. "I'm not letting you marry Daryl. I'm going to be your baby's father…if you'll let me. I love you, Destiny, and I know you love me. Give me a chance to prove to you that you can count on me to always be there for you."

"I should have told you about the baby before we—"

He pressed a finger against her lips. "We all make mistakes," he said. "I let you kick me out, knowing that you wouldn't follow through and take Daryl up on his offer."

"How did you know I wasn't going to marry him?"

"Because you love me."

"I do love you, Buck. But you deserve someone better."

"You're the perfect woman for me."

"I'll try my best to be everything you ever wanted and more."

"The same goes for me, Destiny. I'm going to prove to you that I can be a good father to the baby."

"Just don't leave me, Buck."

"Neither one of us is ever going anywhere without the other. From now on we're stuck like glue." He brushed a knuckle across her cheek. "No more secrets, okay?"

"I promise."

He sealed their fate with a kiss, his ego soaring from the shouts of encouragement of the cowboys cheering them. "What do you say we find someplace more private to make plans for the future?"

"How about Lizard Gulch? Do you think you could be happy living there and working in the garage with me?"

Buck's throat tightened. He knew how important having a real *home* was to Destiny. "Honey, you are my home—I can be happy anywhere as long as I'm with you." He reached for his gear bag and then grabbed her hand. "Now let's go load your bike into the back of my pickup and head home." When they stepped outside into the parking lot, Buck said, "I've always wanted to run my own garage, but I think I've got the better end of the deal helping you run yours."

"Our garage, Buck. We're doing everything together." Destiny went up on tiptoe and kissed him. When she broke off the kiss, she said, "Melba's going to be thrilled to have you back."

"She just wants my help riding herd over all the crazies in town."

They stopped next to her Harley, and Destiny wrapped her arms around Buck's waist and laid her head on his chest. "I love you, Buck."

He grinned.

"I'm not joking," she said. "You're the happy ever after I thought I'd never have."

He hugged her close. "Who would have known that

the afternoon you rescued me from the side of the road you were my Destiny."

"I just want to be sure." Tears filled her eyes. "Will you marry me, Buck Owens Cash?"

He nodded. "'I'll Take a Chance On Loving You.'"

She laughed as she wiped the tears dribbling down her cheeks. "Quoting Buck Owens's music now?"

"You know that song?"

"As soon as I realized you were named for the country-and-western legend, I looked up his songs."

"Oh, yeah?" Buck kissed her—he couldn't help it. She was his now, and he couldn't get enough of her. After a wolf whistle alerted him that he might be getting carried away with Destiny in the parking lot, he ended their kiss then borrowed a ramp from a friend's horse trailer and secured the Harley in his truck bed.

Their whirlwind romance was only beginning, but Buck was sure of one thing—he'd never look at life quite the same way as he had before.

And that's what real love was all about—seeing life in a new light—the light that leads down the road to happy ever after.

Epilogue

"Are you sure about the veil, Destiny?"

"Stop worrying, Violet." Destiny secured the lace to her head. "Buck is my Prince Charming. He'll break the spell on your veil." She hugged the older woman.

"Good, because I have my eye on Bernie's cousin."

Willard Humphrey was ten years younger than Violet and had shown up in town last week with only a suitcase and a dog named Kitty. Destiny had looked out her bedroom window one morning and had spotted the dog resting beneath the tree in the cemetery, Bernie's cats snuggling against its side. Apparently the animals of Lizard Gulch were as peculiar as its residents.

"I'd better make a move on Willard before Melba sinks her claws into the man." Violet stood back and perused Destiny's outfit. "You look beautiful."

Destiny hadn't done anything different to herself, but Buck's love made her feel as if she was the most beautiful woman on earth—at least for today.

Melba poked her head inside the minister's office. "Are you ready?"

"I am." Destiny smoothed her hands down her white leather pants, which she'd barely managed to zip. After she and Buck set the church date, she'd offered to buy a wedding dress, but Buck had insisted she wear the same outfit she'd had on the day they'd first met. Destiny was hard put to deny Buck anything. Next week she'd go to her second appointment at the women's clinic in Kingman, and Buck had asked to tag along with her. Already he acted as if the baby was his son or daughter. Destiny didn't know what she'd done to deserve Buck coming into her life, but she and her child were truly blessed to have his love.

"The chapel's full and it's hot out there," Melba said. "Unless you want folks passing out from heatstroke, you'd better get a move on."

The three women left the office through a side door and walked to the front of the chapel, where Bernie waited to escort her down the aisle.

"You look real nice, Mayor Saunders." Bernie wore his top hat and tux jacket over freshly washed jeans. The scent of coconut hair tonic clashed with the perfumed soap Destiny had used to bathe in earlier in the morning. Dixie had given Destiny a bridal basket of homemade soaps and lotions from her store along with a note from all the Cash women, welcoming her to the family.

Family.

The chapel was packed with Buck's family and most of Lizard Gulch had shown up, too. No one disputed that the residents got the better end of the deal they'd worked out with Custer and Wyndell Resorts—everyone was happy.

Melba waved at Mack, who stood with his guitar next to the pastor at the front of the chapel. A moment later, "Here Comes the Bride" echoed through the small room.

Destiny slid her arm through Bernie's and her gaze

found Buck—he looked so handsome in his suit and polished cowboy boots. Marsha's father had insisted on performing the ceremony, and Pastor Bugler smiled at Destiny as she made the trip down the aisle to the altar.

"Buck Owens Cash," Bernie said, placing her hand in Buck's. "You take good care of our Destiny. She's very special to us." Bernie tapped his finger against his sheriff's badge. "You treat her right or you'll answer to me."

"You have my word that I'll keep Destiny safe and happy." Buck stared into her eyes. "Forever."

"Ladies and gentlemen, we are gathered here today in God's presence to marry Destiny Saunders and Buck Owens Cash." The pastor glanced up at the ceiling and said, "One less Cash brother running loose for fathers to worry about."

"How many brothers are left?" Melba called out from the front pew. "I've got a younger cousin in Alabama that needs a husband."

"My granddaughter just graduated from beauty school in Tucson and—"

"Do they like older women?" A male voice in the back of the chapel traveled across the pews. "I got a sister in Cincinnati who's never been married."

Destiny and Buck locked gazes. "Are you sure, Buck? When you marry me, you're marrying the whole town."

"I'm sure, honey." Buck grinned. "Life in Lizard Gulch will never be boring, that's for sure."

She snuggled against his side and listened to the wedding guests bicker over whose niece, neighbor or daughter should be matched up with Porter and Mack. Pastor Bugler attempted to silence the group, but few paid attention to him.

"Vegas is only two hours away," Buck whispered in her ear.

"I've got a full tank of gas in my Harley," she said.

"We could have Elvis marry us."

The temptation to grab Buck's hand, jump on her bike and ride to Sin City was powerful, but no one would forgive them if they went on the lam and returned to town married a few days later. "We'll celebrate our first anniversary in Vegas," she said.

"Promise?"

Forgetting the wedding guests, Destiny wrapped her arms around Buck's neck. "Buck, I take you for my lawfully wedded husband."

"Destiny, I take you for my lawfully wedded wife."

"Hey, everyone, shut up! Buck and Destiny are marrying themselves!"

"Can they do that?"

"No, stupid, but they're tired of waiting for us to be quiet."

"Well, then, quit talking!"

"Dearly beloved," Pastor Bugler spoke above the voices. "We are gathered here today…"

* * * * *

There are only two Cash brothers still single!
Be sure to look for the next book in
THE CASH BROTHERS *series by Marin Thomas.*
Available in August 2014
wherever Harlequin books are sold.

Available June 3, 2014

#1501 HER COWBOY HERO

The Colorado Cades

by Tanya Michaels

When Colin Cade gets a job on Hannah Shaw's ranch, he doesn't expect her to be so young and beautiful—or to have a little boy who reminds Colin of the one he lost.

#1502 THE TEXAN'S BABY

Texas Rodeo Barons

by Donna Alward

In the first book of a new six-book miniseries, Lizzie Baron feels the need to let loose—and she gets help from Christopher Miller, a sexy saddle bronc rider. But their night together leads to an unexpected result!

#1503 THE SEAL'S BABY

Operation: Family

by Laura Marie Altom

Libby Dewitt, pregnant and alone, brings out the hero in Navy SEAL Heath Stone. But can Libby help him overcome his tragic past and love again?

#1504 A RANCHER'S HONOR

Prosperity, Montana

by Ann Roth

It was only supposed to be one night of fun—after all, day care owner Lana Carpenter and rancher Sly Pettit have nothing in common. Until they discover a connection between them they never could have imagined...

HARCNM0514

REQUEST YOUR FREE BOOKS!
2 FREE NOVELS PLUS 2 FREE GIFTS!

HARLEQUIN

American ★ Romance

LOVE, HOME & HAPPINESS

YES! Please send me 2 FREE Harlequin® American Romance® novels and my 2 FREE gifts (gifts are worth about $10). After receiving them, if I don't wish to receive any more books, I can return the shipping statement marked "cancel." If I don't cancel, I will receive 4 brand-new novels every month and be billed just $4.74 per book in the U.S. or $5.24 per book in Canada. That's a savings of at least 14% off the cover price! It's quite a bargain! Shipping and handling is just 50¢ per book in the U.S. and 75¢ per book in Canada.* I understand that accepting the 2 free books and gifts places me under no obligation to buy anything. I can always return a shipment and cancel at any time. Even if I never buy another book, the two free books and gifts are mine to keep forever.

154/354 HDN F4YN

Name	(PLEASE PRINT)	
Address		Apt. #
City	State/Prov.	Zip/Postal Code

Signature (if under 18, a parent or guardian must sign)

Mail to the **Harlequin® Reader Service:**
IN U.S.A.: P.O. Box 1867, Buffalo, NY 14240-1867
IN CANADA: P.O. Box 609, Fort Erie, Ontario L2A 5X3

Want to try two free books from another line?
Call 1-800-873-8635 or visit www.ReaderService.com.

* Terms and prices subject to change without notice. Prices do not include applicable taxes. Sales tax applicable in N.Y. Canadian residents will be charged applicable taxes. Offer not valid in Quebec. This offer is limited to one order per household. Not valid for current subscribers to Harlequin American Romance books. All orders subject to credit approval. Credit or debit balances in a customer's account(s) may be offset by any other outstanding balance owed by or to the customer. Please allow 4 to 6 weeks for delivery. Offer available while quantities last.

Your Privacy—The Harlequin® Reader Service is committed to protecting your privacy. Our Privacy Policy is available online at www.ReaderService.com or upon request from the Harlequin Reader Service.

We make a portion of our mailing list available to reputable third parties that offer products we believe may interest you. If you prefer that we not exchange your name with third parties, or if you wish to clarify or modify your communication preferences, please visit us at www.ReaderService.com/consumerchoice or write to us at Harlequin Reader Service Preference Service, P.O. Box 9062, Buffalo, NY 14269. Include your complete name and address.

HAR13R

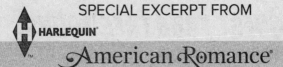
Lizzie Baron pressed the buzzer.

There was a click and then a voice. "Hello?"

"Uh…hi. I'm looking for Christopher Miller?"

"That's me."

"It's…uh…" She scrambled to think of what she'd said to
him that night. "It's Elizabeth."

There was a pause.

"From the bar in Fort Worth."

The words came out strained.

"Come on up."

She could do this. She paused as she got off the elevator.

A door opened and Christopher stepped into the hall. Her feet
halted and she stared at him, her practiced words flying out of
her head.

He was staring at her, too. "It really is you," he said. "What
the hell are you doing here?"

For weeks, Chris had been wondering if he should try to find
out who she was. They'd met at a honky-tonk after a less-than-
stellar rodeo performance on his part. He'd figured he'd nurse
his wounds with a beer and head back to the motel where he was
staying.

And then he'd seen her. He'd ordered another beer, looked
over at her and she'd smiled, and all his brain cells turned
to mush.

When he'd woken the next morning, the bed had been empty. That had been nearly two months ago.

"Elizabeth." He stepped aside so she could enter his apartment.

"Call me Lizzie. Everybody does."

"You didn't say your name was Lizzie the night we met."

"I was trying to be mysterious."

"It worked." He put his hands in his pockets. "How did you find me?"

"Rodeo's a small world."

"You're saying that you got my address from rodeo records?" The blush was back. "Yes."

"Why would you do that?"

"Because I need to talk to you."

Quiet settled through the condo. Whatever she wanted to tell him, she was nervous. Afraid.

And then it hit him upside the head. "Look, do I need to be tested for an STD or something? Is that why you're here?"

"What the hell would give you that idea?"

"Hey, you're the one who disappeared and only gave me your first name. Now you show up weeks later, looking completely different, and say you need to talk to me. If it's not an STD, what the hell…"

His mouth dropped open.

"No," he whispered. "No, it isn't possible. We used condoms."

She looked up, misery etched in every feature. "I assure you it is possible. I'm pregnant, and the baby's yours."

Look for THE TEXAN'S BABY
by Donna Alward in June 2014
wherever books and ebooks are sold.

HARLEQUIN®

American Romance®

To save a SEAL…

Libby Dewitt, pregnant and alone, brings out the hero in navy SEAL Heath Stone. Despite her own troubles, her heart aches at all Heath has been through. To save this SEAL, Libby is ready to fight—for love! But can Libby help him overcome his tragic past and love again?

Look for
The SEAL's Baby
from the *Operation: Family* series

by LAURA MARIE ALTOM
in June 2014 from
Harlequin® American Romance®.
Available wherever books and ebooks are sold.

Also available from the *Operation: Family* series
by Laura Marie Altom:

A SEAL's Secret Baby
The SEAL's Stolen Child
The SEAL's Valentine
A Navy SEAL's Surprise Baby
The SEAL's Christmas Twins

www.Harlequin.com